Termination Dust

a novel by Alana Terry

"All your children will be taught by the LORD, and great will be their peace."

Isaiah 54:13

Note: The views of the characters in this novel do not necessarily reflect the views of the author, nor is their behavior necessarily condoned.

The characters in this book are fictional. Any resemblance to real persons is coincidental. No part of this book may be reproduced in any form (electronic, audio, print, film, etc.) without the author's written consent.

www.alanaterry.com

ALANA TERRY

CHAPTER 1

Kimmie should have never mentioned the funeral home to her stepfather. What had she been thinking?

Maybe it was defiance. Or maybe the grief was keeping her from acting rationally.

"You think I'm made out of money?" Chuck bellowed. "You're just like your mother. That woman was always nagging me, every day of my life. *More, more, more.* It's all she could say."

His voice rose in a mocking falsetto. Kimmie's mother was lying in the morgue, but Chuck continued to mock her heartlessly. "*Honey, we need more grocery money. Honey, we're late on the car payment.* Do you know how much I hated her whining?" He blew his nose then dropped the used paper towel onto the floor.

He and Kimmie both stared at it, a familiar battle of wills as he silently demanded she clean up after him.

She glowered at him.

1

Things were going to be different now. They had to be. Her mother — God rest her soul — had wanted to escape. For years, Mom fed Kimmie dreams of freedom in hushed whispers. "We can go move to your sister's in Anchorage. Meg will take us in."

But Kimmie had learned years earlier not to get her hopes up. Mom wasn't going anywhere. And in her darkest moments, she hated her weakness. Maybe it was Kimmie's fault. If she'd only been more supportive or more courageous, she could have forced Mom to leave. Her sister only lived a four-hour drive away. Mom could have gotten help. She could have been safe.

But Mom refused to run away. She decided to remain trapped here in this trailer, stuck in a life with no other purpose than picking up Chuck's snot-ridden paper towels, heating up his canned chili, opening his bottles of beer. Mom and Kimmie had both stayed, a silent agreement, a vow they never spoke but both understood. Kimmie would never leave her mother. Not here, not with Chuck.

So Mom had taken the only escape she could.

Now Kimmie was free to go. She could walk out that door, show the spunk and self-respect and courage Mom could never manage to conjure up.

That's what she should do. That's what any outside observer

would expect her to do, like that kind trooper who responded to Kimmie's call the day Mom died. Even now, Taylor's soft eyes and soothing voice gave her confidence.

Courage.

You didn't deserve any of this. She could almost hear the trooper whispering the words to her. He was new to the force, not one of the regulars who used to come and do well-child checks when Kimmie was still a minor, back when she was expected to lie away every single bruise and cut on her body.

When Taylor came to her trailer, Kimmie was struck by how young he looked. She was a confused mess after finding her Mom's body in the garage, but he listened to her patiently, even offering to make her tea to help her calm down. The suggestion made her feel like an entirely different person, the kind of person who kept her kitchen stocked with nice things like tea bags and sugar cubes and pretty, matching mugs.

Instead, they settled on lukewarm Cokes.

Kimmie and Taylor had sat at the folding table in the kitchen and talked. Even though the questions were all pointed toward explaining her mother's suicide, she felt like he understood her. Only at one point, Kimmie got flustered when Taylor asked why she stayed at home when nearly everyone else in Glennallen left rural Alaska after high school.

"My mom's not very healthy," she stammered, fumbling over her words. It was difficult to know which tense she was supposed to use as the EMTs were at that same moment preparing to transport her mom's body after cutting her down from the garage rafters. "I've been watching over her."

The real answer, as Kimmie knew, was far more complicated. She thought she recognized in Taylor's eyes an expression of compassion. Understanding.

Did he know what her life was really like? Could he guess?

Maybe it was because he was the only man even close to her age who had spoken to her kindly in years. Or maybe because as a trooper he signified everything Kimmie had been longing for — bravery, confidence, the ability to protect others — that she hadn't stopped thinking about him since that first meeting three days ago.

And now it was Taylor's voice she heard in her head, the same man who sat with her the day her mom died, drinking Coke because as far as Kimmie knew Chuck had never owned a single tea bag in his life. *You didn't deserve any of this.*

Taylor didn't understand. Even if Kimmie wanted a happier life, freeing herself from Chuck wasn't nearly as simple or straight-forward as opening that door and walking down the driveway toward the Glenn Highway, hitching a ride to

Anchorage where her older sister would be ready to take her.

Her stepfather cleared his throat — a wet, phlegmy noise that made Kimmie feel nauseated. Or maybe that was the hunger. When was the last time she'd eaten? Chuck had skipped breakfast and lunch, perhaps dealing with the loss of his wife in his own way. But when Chuck didn't eat, that meant the family didn't eat. Kimmie was older. She was used to hunger pains.

It was harder for Pip.

She'd put her half brother down for his afternoon nap about an hour earlier, sitting on their bed with his head in her lap. Like most days they spent at home instead of at the daycare where she worked, she smoothed Pip's forehead and sang him to sleep. The ditties were the ones her mother taught her, the ones she and Pip both loved, Bible verses set to music. Chuck would throw a fit if he heard them, but some football game was blaring on the TV, drowning out Kimmie's clandestine melody.

And we know that in all things ... all things ... all things ... And we know that in all things God does what's best for those who love him.

It had been one of Kimmie's favorites when she was Pip's age, a time before Chuck, before this drafty trailer, this squalor. A time when Mom looked young and happy, always waiting with open arms for cuddles and hugs, always ready to make up a new song.

And we know that in all things ... all things ... all things ...

With drooping eyelids and cheeks stained with tears, Pip had looked up at her and in his own invented sign language made a flame. The fire song was his favorite, and Kimmie felt her own soul encouraged as she sang him the words.

When you walk through the river, you know I'm with you.

When you pass through the water, I'm right there by your side.

When you walk through the fire, you'll never be burned.

Those flames, they won't set you ablaze.

Maybe Mom's little tune is what gave Kimmie the courage to confront Chuck after Pip was finally asleep. Then again, *confront* was far too strong a word to describe the way she tiptoed into the living room, her heart thudding in her chest, her hands clammy with sweat.

"I think we should have a funeral." She'd been shocked that her voice didn't squeak.

Chuck crushed his beer can and tossed it onto the carpet, hocking a wad of spit in the direction where it fell. "Don't got the money."

Kimmie knew that was a lie. Mom had died the day before her deposit from welfare cleared the bank. Factoring in Chuck's disability payments, Kimmie knew there was money to be had. It usually took Chuck at least ten days into each month to drink through their funds. Besides, her sister could cover any actual expense, but now wasn't the time to rub her stepfather's nose in Meg's success.

"I'm not asking for anything fancy," she persisted, "but you were married for ten years. The least you could do is give her a proper burial."

This time, the loogie Chuck spat landed on the carpet near Kimmie's bare feet. "The witch killed herself. No Christian pastor's gonna bury her, and funeral homes aren't nothing but a rip-off."

"I already called Glennallen Bible." Kimmie had anticipated and was ready for her stepfather's arguments. "The pastor there said he'd be willing to ..."

Chuck pointed the remote at the TV screen and turned up the game until the sound of wildly cheering fans made Kimmie feel as though her teeth were rattling in place. She folded her hands across her chest. "I think it's at least worth considering."

Chuck glowered at her. "You telling me how to take care of my own business?"

She shook her head, but it was too late. Chuck was out of his seat. Kimmie only had time to flinch before he swung out his arm and slapped her hard across the face.

"You talking back to me?"

She set her jaw so he couldn't see her pained expression.

"You're no better than that witch of a mom of yours." He spat in her face, and Kimmie was relieved at the smell of stale beer. When Chuck was drunk, he never bothered to waste too much energy beating her.

He pushed her aside, and she stayed down, praying and hoping he'd be too tired to persist in his fight. Praying and hoping Pip would sleep through his father's rage or at least have the good sense to stay in his room.

Chuck gave Kimmie's back a half-hearted kick then stomped back over to his recliner, flinging several dirty napkins and half a bag of spilled sunflower seeds onto the floor by his feet.

Kimmie didn't mention the idea of a funeral again.

CHAPTER 2

Later that night, Kimmie stared out the window in the bedroom she shared with Pip and listened to her brother's gentle snoring. A full harvest moon rose through her window, providing enough light that she could still see the white tips of the mountains behind the trailer. As a child, Kimmie always loved that first sprinkling of snow on the mountain peaks — the termination dust that signaled the end of summer, the start of a new school year.

She'd been a good student. Even after her widowed mother moved them from Anchorage and into Chuck's trailer when Kimmie was a teen, she had managed to keep up her grades. The Glennallen high school was small, just a little more than two dozen in her class, but Kimmie had been popular enough and respected. She learned how to pretend well enough that, as far as she knew, she never gave anyone reason to suspect what kind of hell she was living through at home.

In a way, those high-school years — riddled though they

were with petty fights, catty gossips, acne breakouts, and nearly paralyzing self-consciousness — were easier than the life she was leading now. School gave her a place to escape, a sanctuary where for seven and a half hours out of every single weekday Kimmie was free from her stepfather's incessant demands, yelling fits, and occasional beatings. That's why seeing the termination dust on the mountains at the end of each August always left Kimmie feeling hopeful.

Free.

But all that was in the past now. Her friends from high school left Glennallen years ago, some to college, others to jobs in Anchorage or the Lower 48. In fact, Kimmie hadn't even graduated with her class. Pip was born over Christmas break during her senior year, and since the delivery left Mom weak and anemic, Chuck decided Kimmie would stay home to help watch over the house and the baby. She earned her GED the same month her friends from high school started moving away from home, mostly for good. Kimmie didn't blame them. How many times had she fantasized about leaving herself?

She and Mom had dreamed about it in scared, hushed whispers in the bedroom while Chuck dozed on his littered reclining chair.

"Meg will take us in," Mom always declared. Kimmie's

older sister was seventeen when Chuck came into the picture, and she had successfully convinced Mom to let her live with her best friend so she could finish her senior year with her class in Anchorage.

Chuck was glad there was one fewer mouth to feed.

As Kimmie quickly learned what kind of man her stepfather was, she dreamed of a home with Meg. A life in Anchorage — and more importantly a life free from Chuck — would make putting up with her sister's infuriating superiority complex worthwhile.

The unfortunate — maybe even pathetic — truth was that Mom was too scared to leave Chuck, and Kimmie was too loyal to leave Mom alone with a monster like him. And so they suffered together, drawing hope from their plans of escape whispered in dark bedrooms while the man who held them captive snored loudly from his easy chair.

And the years passed.

Mom grew gray, then got pregnant. Kimmie dropped out of school, and the baby brother she expected to despise snuggled up against her chest, with little dribbles of milk leaking from the corners of his mouth and gas bubbles that made him look like he was smiling directly at her.

Kimmie was so protective of her little brother, she swore

she'd kill Chuck before letting him harm such a helpless, innocent creature. But as far as she knew, Pip's father had never raised a hand to him, a mystery Kimmie didn't know whether to attribute to their shared genetics or shared gender or maybe even the miraculous answer to all those prayers she'd prayed over Pip when he was a soft newborn who smelled like milk and baby powder.

It took almost a year for Mom to recover from the trauma of her home birth, where she'd been attended only by Kimmie and Chuck, who refused to let any member of the family set foot in a hospital or doctor's office. Even once her body repaired itself, Mom never regained her energy, and the bulk of the parenting fell on Kimmie. Apparently, this was Chuck's plan from the beginning. He wanted Mom free to wait on him, to dump his tin cans of beans and chili into the stove pot every few hours, to keep him in constant supply of sunflower seeds, cold coffee, and freshly opened beer. By the time the condensation no longer glistened on the can, the booze was declared too stale, and Mom was sent to the kitchen to fetch another.

Kimmie strained her ears to listen for Chuck's snoring. Even before Mom's death, he'd stopped sleeping regularly in their room. Apparently, it was much easier to remain in the reclining chair twenty-four hours a day. She was surprised he still made the effort to walk himself to the toilet, an act which comprised the entirety of Chuck's physical activity if you disregarded the exercise he got hitting the members of his family.

All except Pip. God continued to answer Kimmie's prayers for his safety. For her brother's sake, she was grateful. But that also complicated any plans Kimmie might make about her future. Mom was no longer Chuck's hostage. As tragic as her suicide was, Mom was now free. Which meant Kimmie could leave.

But what would happen to Pip?

She turned to look at him, sucking his thumb in his sleep. She should probably discourage the habit, but tonight she didn't have the energy or the will. Pip was so young. Too young to lose a mom. Younger even than Kimmie had been when her father died. She didn't have any memories of her dad. One of her biggest fears was that Pip would forget their mom entirely.

How do you keep someone's memory alive? How do you keep a child from growing up and forgetting entirely? Kimmie had lost track of how many times as a kid she said or thought something like, *my Dad died when I was four, but it's not that big of a deal because I didn't really know him.*

How could she have been so wrong? About her father, about

everything? If Mom were here, Kimmie might ask. Not about her father. That subject was clearly off-limits for as long as they lived under Chuck's roof. But what was Kimmie supposed to do now, especially without Mom's guidance?

She stared out the window. Wispy clouds had drifted in and found their way just below the full moon, which lent them an eerie glow. Kimmie didn't believe in ghosts. The only afterlife she trusted in was the picture of heaven Mom had taught her from her earliest years. She was supposed to feel happy for Mom, now free from her suffering, free from her life held prisoner to Chuck.

A siren wailed from the Glenn Highway. Kimmie thought about Taylor, the kind trooper who'd shared Cokes with her in the kitchen just a few days earlier.

What was he doing now? Did he think of her? What would he say if he knew what Kimmie's life was really like? What would he do?

Pip made a little whimper in his sleep. Kimmie pulled back his tattered blanket, crawled onto the mattress next to him, and stared at the wall where the harvest moon cast dancing shadows from the drifting clouds outside.

CHAPTER 3

Kimmie woke up to a crisp autumn morning. She and Pip had been clutching each other in their sleep, whether from the cold or the sheer loneliness of their existence and the grief they both shared.

She slid out of bed, careful not to wake him, and peeked out the bedroom door. Chuck was still asleep in his recliner, but the quiet and peace of the morning wouldn't last long. If she was lucky, she'd have time for a shower without hearing her stepfather yell about all the money she wasted running the hot water.

Maybe if he fixed all the stupid leaks in this cheap trailer, she wouldn't be so cold all the time and need to thaw herself out under the scalding flow.

Kimmie had taken these past few days off from work, but they needed her back at the daycare soon. One of her coworkers had recently moved away — no one knew where — and Kimmie and her friend Jade were now the only reliable staff.

Kimmie had mixed feelings about returning to work. On the one hand, since Chuck had refused to offer her mother even the simplest of funerals, there wasn't a whole lot for her to do at home. No relatives coming to visit. Her sister Meg would take care of the body in Anchorage, and since Meg was married to a real estate agent with enough money to pay for a five-bedroom home on the hillside and two or three tropical vacations a year, Kimmie figured Meg would find a way to give their mom a nice burial even if Chuck wouldn't let them plan a formal service.

It wasn't right. Mom had been the most faithful, God-fearing woman Kimmie ever knew. And now she was gone, without a single pastor to pray over her gravesite or a gathering of friends to share memories from her life. Kimmie wondered if Mom still had any friends in Anchorage, if Meg would find anyone to attend a service in her honor.

Everything about the past week felt wrong. Surreal. Like a badly written script where none of the characters acted like themselves. A knock-off of real life, poorly written and unnecessarily tragic. Kimmie kept waiting for the director to stop the cameras and rant about the terrible quality of the plot, the cheap acting, and the senseless scenes.

Kimmie tiptoed into the bathroom, careful not to wake Chuck up. While she waited for the water to heat up, she stretched in front of the smudged mirror. Mom had been a prisoner, leaving the trailer to go to the grocery store and back and that was all. So she'd developed an entire morning calisthenics routine, and when Kimmie was younger, she'd watch her mother exercise in unmasked adoration. Sometimes Mom would sing her Bible songs while she stretched and worked her muscles.

Whatever you do, work at it with all your heart, since you're working for God and not for men.

Above all else, love each other deeply, deeply, deeply, for love covers over a multitude of sins.

Kimmie took off her pajamas and stepped into the shower, wincing as the hot water scalded her skin. She'd only have two or three minutes before Chuck would be pounding on the door, snarling at her to turn that cursed shower off, but for right now she could enjoy the quiet and solitude.

She could stand under the steaming spray as the heat melted away her icy chill.

She could pretend, if only for a moment, that Mom was in the kitchen, brewing Chuck's coffee, preparing the family's breakfast. She could hear her mom's faint humming in the echoes of her memories.

Above all else, love each other deeply, deeply, deeply, for love covers over a multitude of sins.

If only Mom had realized sooner that sometimes not even love itself is enough to save you.

CHAPTER 4

Kimmie hoped the rest of the morning would pass smoothly. Some days her stepfather was tired enough that he left Kimmie and Pip alone. Chuck had never said so, but it was tacitly understood that all the chores now fell on Kimmie since Mom wasn't here to do them. After her shower, she wrapped her hair up in a towel and headed to the kitchen to start on Chuck's coffee.

"What you all dressed up for?" He was already at the folding table in the dining room, sitting before a dirty, empty mug. A painted picture of the Grand Canyon chipped away from its enamel.

Kimmie glanced down at her jeans and sweater. "I'm going back to the daycare today." He must have remembered. Since Chuck's trailer didn't have a landline or any cell reception, Kimmie's coworker Jade had stopped by the house yesterday to beg her to return to work. Chuck had been in the middle of a half-drunk, half-naked outburst even though it wasn't even

19

dinnertime yet. Kimmie had been embarrassed, more on Jade's behalf than anything else.

"When you gonna be home?" Even when he wasn't drunk, Chuck had the tendency to slur all his syllables together, making the noises that took the least amount of muscle control or mental effort.

"Three," Kimmie answered, "like normal."

Chuck's biggest stipulation when it came to Kimmie's work at the daycare was that she clocked out before the school-aged kids got dropped off. Pip always went with her, and Chuck didn't want his son picking up bad habits or germs from the elementary-aged students. Every once in a while, his demands left the center with an uncomfortable staffing predicament, but Chuck was resolute. The day Kimmie and Pip came home at 3:08 instead of 3:07 would be the day her stepfather marched to the daycare himself and told her coworkers she quit. He'd made that threat multiple times, and Kimmie knew he'd follow through. Since the daycare got her out of the house, and more importantly gave Pip the chance to play with kids his age and toys besides crushed beer cans and spilled sunflower seeds, Kimmie would do anything in her power to keep her job.

Even placate her stepfather, whose bare stomach bulged over his flannel pants as he sat half-dressed at the table, waiting for his food.

She grabbed two slices of white bread and threw them into the toaster. While she reached for the coffee, Chuck mumbled something.

"What'd you say?" she asked.

He glowered at her, as if her inability to understand his pronouncement was a reflection of her own mental incompetence instead of his embarrassingly poor diction. "I said I'm gonna need you home now. No more daycare for you."

Kimmie had been prepared for this conversation and was actually surprised it took four whole days until he brought it up. Thankfully the extra time gave her plenty of time to fine-tune her argument. She wouldn't go into details about how the daycare was such a better environment for Pip and might even help him to start talking in full sentences soon. There was no reason to appeal to Chuck's fatherly nature since he didn't possess any at all, so she answered Chuck in the language he understood best.

"We won't be getting Mom's welfare anymore. I was thinking if I kept working at the daycare, I could help with the budget." Kimmie was treading dangerous waters. There was no way Chuck could concede to being dependent on an uneducated girl in her twenties, but she also knew that the fool was capable of doing simple math and had to realize he couldn't afford all that booze on his disability payments alone.

She held her breath, waiting for a response, not knowing if her stepfather would reluctantly give in or begin a loud and obnoxious tirade that was certain to wake up Pip. For years, she'd tried to stash away little bits of pocket change from her paycheck, storing up a small but treasured cache of one- and five-dollar bills. She'd imagined it might eventually turn into enough to convince her mom to take Pip and leave. It wasn't living expenses they needed. As snobby as her sister and her rich Anchorage husband might be, they wouldn't turn away their own flesh and blood. Mom's biggest fear had been that Chuck would demand to keep Pip. Even though there was no court in the nation that should award someone like Chuck sole custody, Mom wouldn't leave without enough money to hire the best lawyer in Alaska just to be sure.

Kimmie never mentioned her plans, but Mom found out about the extra money lying around. Toward the end of each month, when Pip hadn't eaten a hot meal at home in weeks and Chuck was bellowing for more beer, her mom would sneak into her room and whisper, "Don't you have a little something? Just to hold us over a few more days?"

And so Kimmie would relinquish the ones and the fives

she'd managed to stash away. Eventually, Chuck realized what she was doing. From that point on, he made her sign her paychecks over to him.

At present, Kimmie had $2.23, all in change, to her name, which she kept hidden beneath the torn lining of one of her winter snow boots.

From his spot at the table, her stepfather glowered at her. He was probably straining to do the calculations, figuring out if having a fulltime slave to wait upon his every need was worth giving up so he wouldn't have to live off his disability alone.

"Home by three," he grumbled. He slammed his empty mug on the table and then slid it toward Kimmie to fill with the black sludge he called his morning coffee. "And no school holidays."

Kimmie turned her back to him, figuring that now was not the time to let her stepfather see her smile.

As long as she and Pip had that job at the daycare, that job away from Chuck, she could plan. She could scheme. She could call her sister from Jade's cell phone and beg her to come and pick her up.

Pick her and Pip up, actually.

How a girl Kimmie's age with no real job experience, no education, and no future prospects could assume guardianship of her half-brother against the wishes of his biological parent still remained what seemed like an insurmountable impossibility, but as long as she got those few hours alone with Pip each day without Chuck's constantly surveying every move she made, she was going to figure something out.

She had to.

CHAPTER 5

After Kimmie fixed her stepdad's breakfast, she added his dirty dishes to the ever-growing pile in the sink and then went back to her room to wake up Pip. Working the morning shift meant that she and her brother could count on both a hot breakfast and lunch in a single day. There probably weren't all that many nutrients in the microwave croissant sandwiches or canned SpaghettiOs they served at the daycare, but calories were calories. At least Kimmie's job gave her brother more to live off of than the sunflower seed shells his father spat onto the floor.

She knelt on the mattress, leaned over her brother, and nuzzled Pip's ticklish neck with her nose. "Wake up, Buster. We get to play today."

Pip rolled over and blinked at her, his expression momentarily vacant until his face broke out in a cautious smile.

"You ready to go back to work with me?" she asked.

Pip grunted, and Kimmie spent a few minutes she didn't

really have snuggling with him in bed, breathing in his fresh morning smell that still managed to feel clean even though she could never wash him without his throwing a fit.

She pulled out some of Pip's clothes and watched him struggle for his independence before helping him take off his pajamas and get dressed. A few minutes later, they were on their own, making the walk to work. An icy wind stole its way through their thin jackets. She took hers off and wrapped it around Pip to provide an extra layer of warmth.

Hiding her hands in her sweater sleeves to better protect them from the cold, Kimmie gestured toward the mountains. "See that, Buster? See the snow on the mountain tops?"

Pip's eyes widened slightly, Kimmie's only indication he had heard her. At home, Chuck hated any loud noise that didn't come from his own body or his television set. In addition, he was convinced that Pip's speech delays meant he was stupid, and he berated Kimmie anytime he caught her talking to her brother, certain that his mute son was incapable of comprehension.

After being cooped up in the house with Chuck for the past four days, Kimmie realized how freeing it was now to be able to speak clearly.

"Did I ever tell you what the first snow on the mountains is called?" she asked. Pip had been distracted by a car speeding down the Glenn and was no longer staring at the Chugach range in the distance, but Kimmie was grateful to have found her voice again and continued on with her explanation.

"We call it termination dust because it looks like someone sprinkled white dust on the tips of the mountains. *Termination* means ending, and the first snow tells us that summer has ended and winter will be coming soon."

She glanced down at her brother, trying to gauge how much of her explanation he might have understood. He was focused on the way her jacket sleeves hung down by his side, nearly dragging on the ground behind him. She bent down, tied the sleeves loosely together, and kissed his cheek. One of the hardest parts about Pip's speech delay meant that Kimmie was always wondering if her brother understood just how much she loved him. How she'd do anything within her power to protect him.

Even die.

Even kill.

CHAPTER 6

Kimmie stepped into the Glennallen daycare and held the door open for her brother. Before Pip was past the threshold, Kimmie was wrapped up in Jade's arms as her friend attempted to squeeze all the breath out of her lungs.

"I'm so sorry about what happened."

Kimmie didn't know why the reaction surprised her. Knowing what she did about Jade, she shouldn't have expected anything different. Jade was effervescent, extroverted, and probably twice as strong as Kimmie would ever be. Her hug of condolence was as smothering as it was compassionate.

Once freed, Kimmie took a step back. "Thanks. It's good to be back." She helped her brother escape from his layers of coats, pulled out his favorite tub of matchbox cars, then followed Jade into the kitchen.

"What are we making for breakfast this morning?"

Jade held up the Pillsbury can. "Cinnamon rolls."

Kimmie's stomach gurgled. She hoped Jade didn't hear.

28

Kimmie kept the door to the play area propped open so she could supervise the few kids in attendance and suddenly felt sheepish. She'd been so focused on her and Pip's grief over the past few days she'd hardly thought about Jade's visit yesterday. What kind of impression did Jade have of her and her family now? With a stepdad who lazed around the house all day belching out his beer and stripped half naked, a half-brother who refused to speak, and a mom who killed herself ...

She caught Jade staring at her and felt herself blush. Oh, well. Jade never seemed to have a problem speaking her mind or interacting with other people who did. Kimmie took in a deep breath. "I'm really sorry if my stepdad made you uncomfortable when you came over. He's ..."

She struggled for the right words. *He's always like that, sometimes even worse? He's a monster of a man, and I wish he was the one who died instead of my mom?*

She calmed her quivering voice and explained, "He's got a lot to deal with right now." Why was she making excuses for him? Because otherwise she'd have to find a way to explain why she was still living with the beast when she was free to walk away.

Theoretically free, at least.

Kimmie was already starting to feel just as trapped as her

mom had been. There had to be a way to distance herself from her stepfather without abandoning Pip. Maybe she could ask for more hours at the daycare. Then at least she and Pip would be here instead of at home. It would mean more money for Chuck's drinking, and he'd have the trailer to himself ...

But that was the problem. He didn't want the trailer to himself. He wanted someone to pick up all his stained napkins and snot-covered paper towels, someone to fetch his coffee and make sure his beers stayed icy-cold. The man at the funeral home told Kimmie by phone it was natural for people who'd lost a loved one to suicide to feel angry at the deceased, but initially she'd balked at the suggestion. How could she be mad at her mom? For all of Kimmie's begging and pleading, it had become apparent that only dying would free Mom from her servitude. In Kimmie's most honest musings, she'd feared that one day Chuck's anger could lead to murder, and she was relieved that Mom had met death on her own terms.

Mom's suicide was a small act of defiance against a man who'd held her in terror for years. But now Kimmie wished she could take her mom by the shoulders, force her to observe exactly what her death had done. Kimmie was even more trapped than she'd been a week ago. All of Mom's responsibilities now fell on her, and even though Kimmie hated to admit it, Chuck wasn't the only one worrying about how they'd keep the family afloat without those regular welfare payouts.

Worst of all were her worries over Pip. How could a three-year-old understand the finality of death? And since he didn't speak, Kimmie had no idea what he was thinking. Did he figure Mom had abandoned him? That she stopped loving him and ran away? Pip hadn't cried any more than normal these past few days, and even though it seemed like he clutched Kimmie more closely at night, it could also be that she was the one clinging to him.

"He doing all right?" Jade's voice came from right behind Kimmie's shoulder, making her jump. She realized she'd spent the past several minutes staring at her brother. While Jade's little girl and the other early arrivers grouped in the main area coloring or playing in the massive dollhouse that once belonged to Jade's daughter, Pip was in the corner by the cubbies, right where Kimmie had left him. Instead of racing his cars up and down the carpet like most kids would, he focused all his attention on lining them up in concentric circles. Kimmie knew that if she got closer she'd see he'd organized them by color or size or model or whatever other system caught his fancy today.

She forced herself to smile. "Yeah, it's hard on him, but

he's handling things really well."

"Does he understand what happened?"

Kimmie didn't know if Jade was asking about their mom's death in general or her suicide specifically. She shrugged and offered a noncommittal, "It's hard to say."

"How did he do at the funeral? Was that pretty rough on him?"

Kimmie's face grew hot. How could she explain that her stepdad was so heartless he wouldn't even allow them to plan a service?

The oven timer dinged, distracting Jade and freeing Kimmie from the conversation that was destined to grow more awkward the longer it dragged on.

"Cinnamon rolls are ready!" Jade called out. Jade's daughter and the other children cheered and clamored and caused a minor stampede in an effort to be the first seated at the kitchen table. Pip, on the other hand, frowned at the box of cars, studying them as if they were Einstein's theory of relativity, then made a careful selection. He held the truck up, squinting as he turned it around to examine it from all angles before adding it to his circle of cars, perfectly placed and impeccably lined up.

CHAPTER 7

The daycare was quieter than normal, with the Cole twins out with strep throat and another child whose family was on vacation in the Lower 48. The comparable calm was a mixed blessing. With the grief of losing her mom sitting at the base of her neck like a thirty-pound backpack, Kimmie was grateful that today's crowd seemed fairly content to play with only minimal need for supervision. On the other hand, the minutes seemed to drag by as slowly as the Alaskan sunset on the summer solstice.

After breakfast, Pip beelined right back to his toy cars, working himself into an angry panic when he discovered one of his trucks kicked out of place. Kimmie finally managed to calm him, but she had a few new scratches on her arm for her efforts.

As far as fits went, this one was relatively calm. Once Pip was contentedly absorbed in his sorting work again, Kimmie made her way back to the kitchen where Jade was scrubbing down the table with disinfectant.

"Have you made any coffee yet?"

Jade glanced up from her work. "No, you go ahead. I could use a cup myself."

Kimmie hated coffee until she started working at the daycare. Jade showed her the difference between a nice fresh roast and the generic stuff Chuck always bought. Kimmie was also pleasantly surprised to discover that her coffee didn't have to be so strong it poured out like sludge and that a little bit of flavored creamer made a big difference in cutting back on the bitter taste.

Keeping partial attention on the kids playing in the common room, Kimmie pulled down the bag of Alaskan coffee and changed out the old filter.

"What time is it?" Jade asked.

Kimmie glanced at the clock above the sink. "9:45."

"Is it me, or is this day dragging on?"

Kimmie was glad she wasn't the only one who felt that way. A few minutes later, the two women were sitting in rocking chairs on the far side of the playroom with steaming mugs of freshly brewed Kaladi Brothers coffee in their chipped mugs.

"Here's to you." Jade held her cup high. "With prayers for peace and comfort for you and your family after all you've gone through."

Kimmie had never seen anyone make a toast with a mug of coffee before, but she appreciated Jade's thoughtfulness. Taking a small sip, she scanned the room to make a quick mental count of the kids. Jade's daughter Dez was playing by the dollhouse, Noah was coloring at the kiddie table. The Abbot brothers and their cousin Chinook were climbing up and down the small indoor kiddie gym, pretending to be pirates.

"We'll have to get ready for story time pretty soon. You want me to do it today?" Jade asked.

In the past, Kimmie took on reading duty. The kids loved to hear her do her voices, and Kimmie appreciated their enthusiasm and rapture. "I don't mind," she said. "I'll do it."

Jade glanced at her with what looked like the start of a question in her expression, but instead of saying anything she just took another sip of coffee. "That works for me," she said. "I've got to go disinfect that bathroom at some point anyway."

Kimmie would never complain about working with someone who would rather scrub toilets than read a few books out loud. They both finished their coffee, and while Jade helped the kids who needed assistance in the bathroom, Kimmie picked out a few books.

Everyone loved Dr. Seuss, and reading his books had become so second nature Kimmie could do it with only investing a small chunk of her mental energy. Another one of her personal favorites was *There's a Monster at the End of this Book*, but she wasn't sure she had the energy today. She had to get the voice just right to make it sound scary enough to keep everyone amused without actually frightening any of the littler kids. Kimmie had no guidebook on grief, but she suspected that the sooner she could get back to doing all the things she did before, the sooner she could say she had finally moved on.

With the monster book in her hand and a few other especially funny ones thrown in for good measure, she pulled the rocking chair to the center of the playroom.

"All right, guys," she called out, wondering if her voice sounded natural. "Grab your magic carpet square and let's read some stories."

Noah came running first, eager to grab his favorite spot right in front of Kimmie. Chinook sat next to Dez, and the two girls giggled when one of the Abbot boys tripped over an untied shoe.

Everyone was here except for Pip. Kimmie glanced at the bathroom. Had Jade taken him to the toilet?

She leaned forward and laid the books out on the floor in a colorful spread. "All right, guys, if you promise not to touch these or fight about them, I want you to think about which story you want to read first. When I get back you can each tell me your choice and we'll take a vote."

Even before she got out of her chair, she realized she'd set the kids up for failure by making them promise not to fight. She hurried toward the bathroom. Jade was leaning over the toilet, yellow rubber gloves on her hands and hot pink earbuds on her ears. She glanced up. "Need anything?"

Kimmie peeked behind the bathroom door as if her brother might be hiding there. "Have you seen Pip?"

Jade took off her gloves and paused whatever she was listening to on her phone.

"What?"

Kimmie repeated her question, then glanced back at the circle of kids, half expecting him to have joined the group.

"I'm sure he's around here somewhere." Jade's statement of the obvious only made Kimmie's hands clammier.

"I'll check the kitchen," Kimmie said. "Can you see if he went to the nap room for some reason?"

Jade tossed her rubber gloves onto the sink, and Kimmie glanced at her brother's box of cars by the front door. Where had he gone?

She poked her head into the kitchen. "Pip?" After glancing under the table and sink, she checked the broom closet and even the lower cupboards.

"I didn't see him in the nap room." Jade licked her lips. Kimmie knew she wasn't in a strong enough emotional state to determine the exact time to freak out, so she took her cues from her friend.

Jade fingered her chin, glancing sideways. "Think he could have gone outside?"

"I'll go check." Kimmie hurried toward the exit. He knew he wasn't allowed to play outside by himself, and most of the time he was terrified to be away from Kimmie even for a few minutes.

She glanced at his cubby. If he had gone outside, he'd forgotten his coat. Where could he be?

Her heart started pumping wildly, and she didn't know if the surge of terror she felt was a rational reaction or not. How could she? She'd never lost her brother before. In fact, until last summer when he discovered his love of matchbox cars, he'd hardly ever let Kimmie out of a five-foot radius from wherever he was.

"Pip?" A cold blast of air confronted her when she stepped outside. It didn't make sense. Pip was the kind of kid who threw fits when anything in the daily routine changed in even the slightest detail, a kid who had until recently refused to be away from his sister's side while she was at work. Why would he have gone onto the playground by himself?

"Pip!"

She leaned down, peeking in all the tube slides, checking and double-checking anywhere a three-year-old Pip's size could conceivably hide. The choices were fairly limited. Two minutes later she was back in the daycare building, and Jade's nervous shaking of the head revealed that her search had been just as fruitless.

Kimmie's breath grew short. The daycare began to spin in her periphery.

Her brother was lost.

CHAPTER 8

Kimmie stood paralyzed in the entrance to the daycare.

Pip … lost?

It didn't make sense. The concept was too complicated for her brain to register or compute.

He couldn't be lost. He was playing a game. That's what this was. Of course, he was the only kid in preschool who never caught on to hide-and-seek, but maybe he'd finally figured it out and wanted to prove how well he could do it.

"Pip!" Kimmie called out, her voice infused with false cheer.

The children stared at her from their seats in the reading circle.

"Maybe we should do the books later," Jade suggested, and Kimmie couldn't figure out why her co-worker was worried about story time when her brother was missing.

"Pip!" Kimmie hurried to the nap room, retracing the steps Jade must have made just a few minutes earlier. "Pip?"

Her voice was shaky. Uncertain. So were her tentative steps. Was she worried that she'd trip over her brother if she weren't careful? He wasn't that tiny. He couldn't have turned invisible.

"Pip!" She tried not to sound irritated. Wasn't that some sort of dog-training rule? She couldn't remember where she'd heard it. If your dog takes off, don't sound angry or he'll be scared to come back to you. She forced herself to smile. Made her voice higher than natural. "Pip?"

Nothing.

Back to the bathrooms, running now. What if Jade left out the cleaning supplies, and her brother got into them? She flung open the door. No Pip.

She ran back outside, onto the playground then past the daycare fence. Searching everywhere, racing through the parking lots, haphazardly running up the side street. He wouldn't have come all the way out here, would he? And why hadn't she seen him? Was she so busy drinking her coffee she stopped paying attention? Or had she gotten complacent, convinced he would never voluntarily move away from his box of cars? Was she just as guilty as Chuck, who thought that since Pip didn't talk he was incapable of making decisions for himself? Of having an opinion?

Where could he have gone?

She was sprinting now but halted at a stop sign on top of the hill. There was no way Pip was all the way out here. Not without his coat. Not without her. He was scared of just about everything.

Including being alone.

She spun around. She had to find him.

Racing downhill was harder than running up, when the rush of adrenaline helped her defy gravity. Her early sprint had been fueled by the hope that she might find her brother and catch up to him. But she couldn't dawdle now. She had to keep looking. Couldn't slow down.

She pictured him lost and alone, wandering alongside the Glenn Highway. Maybe he'd gotten hurt and freaked out. Maybe he ran into the woods behind the daycare, scared and bleeding. Or worse, what if someone grabbed him? She would have heard if someone came into the daycare, but what if Pip wandered off and was at this moment in the back seat with some predator ...

She wanted to throw up. Emptying her stomach would at least make more room for her stinging lungs and racing heart. She hurried back toward the daycare, praying Jade had found him. Something was wrong. Something in the parking lot.

A trooper's car? What did that mean? Had Jade called the

dispatcher to report a missing child? Or what if it was even worse? What if Pip had tried to cross the Glenn? What if he'd been hit by a car? What if ...

"Don't you work here?" asked a tall man in his crisp, blue trooper uniform.

She knew that voice, but she was so distraught she had a hard time placing it.

He stretched out his hand. "Taylor Tanner. Nice to see you again."

Warmth rushed through her as his palm touched hers, loosening her voice. "I'm so glad you came. I don't know what happened. He was with the cars all morning ..."

He stared at her quizzically, and she realized she was about to start crying. It was too much. Couldn't God see that? Too much. First her mom's death, then Pip getting lost, now this trooper looking at her with so much compassion and empathy.

"Kimmie! Is that you?" Jade called from the open doorway. "Come on in. We found him."

Breath rushed back into her lungs, and she was too relieved to acknowledge the trooper's questioning expression. She ran past him and into the daycare. Falling onto her knees at the sight of Pip, she wrapped her arms around her brother, burying her face into his dinosaur T-shirt.

"He crawled into the dollhouse," Jade explained. "Poor thing must be exhausted. I found him in there taking a nap."

Pip looked at Kimmie. It was rare that she could be entirely sure what he was thinking or feeling, but if she had to guess, right now she'd say he looked scared. "It's okay," she told him. "I'm just glad you're safe."

She studied his face. What was he looking at? She glanced over her shoulder.

"Oh, right." She stood and faced the trooper. "Thanks for stopping by. I guess we've got everything under control. I'm so sorry we bothered you."

His gentle smile spoke of both bemusement and curiosity.

"Trooper Taylor's come here to talk to the kids about stranger safety. Remember?" Jade was staring at Kimmie as if those words should make an ounce of sense. "We talked about it at our last ..." She stopped herself. "Oh, right. You weren't there. You mean I didn't mention it to you this morning?"

Kimmie shook her head.

"Well, that's what's on the schedule for today. Kids," Jade called out, "I want you to grab your magic squares one last time, and we're all going to listen to Trooper Taylor. He's come all the way over here today to talk to us about staying safe, so I know you're all going to put on your listening ears and give him your full attention, right?"

Kimmie was glad for the commotion to get Taylor's focus off of her. She was glad that Jade was here to take charge and tell the children what to do. More than anything, she was glad to have her brother here, safe and sound. He'd never played near that big dollhouse before. Maybe it was a good sign. Maybe it was a positive step forward in his development if he was starting to show interest in something other than his cars.

The kids were staring at Taylor with rapt attention, and Kimmie realized they were quieter and more disciplined than she'd ever seen them. Even Pip had grabbed his carpet square and was sitting down quietly with the others.

Kimmie pulled one of the rocking chairs behind the semi-circle of kids and sank down into it. With the trooper maintaining the children's entire focus, maybe Kimmie could take the next few minutes to decompress.

Maybe she could finally relax.

CHAPTER 9

Jade stood in front of the circle of carpet squares, clapping her hands together to hold everyone's attention. "All right, students, what do we tell Officer Taylor for coming to speak to us today?"

A melancholy chorus of *thank yous* sounded around the room. The children were dismissed for playtime. Jade stepped up to Kimmie. "I'll get lunch ready if you're all right handling things out here."

Kimmie's eyes were on the trooper. Taylor had stopped to help Jade's daughter tie her light-up shoes. "Hmm?"

"I said I'll get lunch ready," Jade repeated. "That okay with you?"

Kimmie pried her eyes away from the touching scene. "Yeah. Sounds good. You need help?"

Jade shook her head. She looked as if she were about to say something, then just shrugged and walked off. Kimmie scanned the room to make sure she kept better track of her brother. Pip was by the dollhouse again, watching two girls playing make-believe. Maybe he really was starting to move past those cars. It would be a huge step forward for him. She just hoped that Chuck would never find out if his son liked to play with dolls.

"It's Kimberly, right?"

She let out a surprised, "Oh," when she realized Taylor was standing right next to her.

"Kimberly?" he repeated.

She nodded, flustered. Hadn't he already left? "Kimmie," she told him. "Or Kimberly. Whichever you prefer."

She cleared her throat and pulled her eyes away from his, focusing again on Pip. Her heart was starting to swell. He'd never shown an interest in imaginative play before, and with what limited knowledge she'd gleaned from the daycare's scarce resources on child development, she knew make-believe was a huge milestone in cognitive development. What if he actually picked up one of those dolls and started to play with it? For the first time, she realized why all those daycare moms and dads were obsessed with carrying their smartphones around to get pictures commemorating all their children's proud achievements.

Jade's daughter noticed Pip staring at her. Kimmie was afraid she'd say something mean and braced herself to jump in and intervene. Instead, Dez held out the doll. Pip stared, and Kimmie held her breath, waiting to see if he'd reach out for it.

"He's a cutie." The trooper's words yanked Kimmie back to reality. He smiled down at her, and she flushed.

Taylor held her gaze. "I just wanted to tell you again how sorry I am about your mom. How's the little one taking it?"

Kimmie glanced at her brother again. He'd taken the doll but just stared at it as if he weren't certain what exactly it was doing in his grasp.

"He's all right," Kimmie answered, and then fearing that her answer sounded too dismissive added, "all things considered."

Taylor nodded as if he understood exactly what she meant, which would be a small miracle seeing how Kimmie didn't even know what she was saying. *How is he? All things considered?* How was a three-year-old supposed to act and feel and think after his mom commits suicide to free herself from an abusive husband? Kimmie felt her hands balling into fists. At least anger gave her a sense of power, however false. It was far more comfortable to feel fury than grief. She couldn't pinpoint who or what she was mad at — her mother for killing herself, her stepfather for being a monster of a human being who couldn't even make his own coffee sludge, God for allowing so many misfortunes to steal away any chance Kimmie had for hope or joy. Maybe even the earth itself for continuing to exist and spin and function normally even though Kimmie's entire world had been shattered.

Taylor cleared his throat, and Kimmie braced herself for some kind of senseless remark — *all things happen for a reason,* or some other unhelpful platitude like that. Instead, he held her gaze and said, "You know, if I'd have known you'd be working here today, I would have planned things differently. I was going to stop by your house a little later this afternoon. I need to talk to you. It's important."

Something flopped inside her gut, and she was pretty sure it had nothing to do with Taylor's kind features, his intense stare, and his perfectly pressed navy-blue uniform.

Pretty sure, but not positive.

Danger signals zinged through her brain, and she braced herself for some terrible blow. The state had decided Pip wasn't being cared for well enough and was going to take him away to be raised by strangers. That had to be it. Why else would he look at her with that apologetic stare?

"I have to head back to the office before long, but do you have a few minutes? I'd love to find a quiet place to talk."

CHAPTER 10

If Taylor expected to find anything resembling privacy here, he'd obviously never spent much time in a daycare. Fortunately, Jade announced that lunch was ready a few minutes later. Kimmie and Taylor could talk in the playroom while Jade served up the kids in the kitchen. Kimmie pulled out the rocking chair, and Taylor sat on top of the coloring table. Kimmie didn't have the heart to ask him to move, and she hoped none of the kids would come out and see the trooper in uniform breaking one of the daycare rules.

Taylor strummed his fingers on his thigh and looked perfectly at ease. Kimmie just wished he could lend her a fraction of his calm and self-possession.

"I wanted to talk to you about your mom."

Kimmie felt her breath whooshing out her lungs. It was hard to tell if his words left her more surprised or relieved, but at least it didn't have to do with Pip.

She had a hard time knowing where to look and found her

eyes flitting between Taylor's black shiny boots, the glistening gold badge on his chest, and the tiny hint of stubble accenting a strongly defined jawline.

"This is a little awkward." Taylor's words belied his demeanor, which remained perfectly casual. "We've had a few discussions at the station that have caused us to look a little bit deeper into your mother's case."

Kimmie stared from his boots to his badge and back down again. What was he saying? Was her family in trouble because her mother killed herself?

Taylor looked over his shoulder. The door to the kitchen was closed, and the empty playroom suddenly felt very large and very quiet.

He lowered his voice. "I hate to be the one to bring this up, but I thought given the circumstances it might be best to talk to you first instead of going to your dad."

Kimmie wanted to correct his mistake, but the word *stepfather* died on her lips before she could speak it.

"I can't go into details, and I know this is obviously a sensitive topic. I just wanted to give you a little warning so you aren't surprised."

She had no idea what he was saying. She had no idea how she was expected to respond. When had people stopped speaking in plain English?

She pried her eyes away from his badge and stared at her hands which fidgeted in her lap. "I'm afraid I don't really understand."

He smiled at her and apologized. "I guess I was being kind of vague. I don't want to sound like an alarmist or anything, but there's something I think you should know."

Time, breath, even her pulse stood still while she waited. Taylor leveled his gaze and didn't say a word until she managed to raise her eyes to meet his.

"There's a chance they're going to open up an investigation looking into your mother's death."

Kimmie understood the individual words but not their coherent meaning when strung together. What was he saying?

Taylor must have sensed her confusion. He let out a sigh, leaned forward, and explained, "We're starting to think this might not have been a suicide after all."

CHAPTER 11

A moment later, Taylor returned from the kitchen and held out a Dixie cup full of tepid water, which Kimmie sipped in miniature installments.

"I'm sorry," he said. "I should have waited to find a better time to talk."

She stared at him, trying once more to piece together the meaning of his words. A dozen different questions jumbled in her brain, but she couldn't focus on a single one long enough to ask it. She replayed everything she remembered about that horrible day. Stepping into the garage, the surreal grisliness of it all. Shouting for her stepdad, tackling Pip to keep him from coming in, waiting for what felt like hours for the troopers and ambulance crew to arrive.

Not a suicide ...

"Other members of the family have raised a few questions."

This time his words' meaning came to Kimmie clearly.

"You mean my sister?" Who else would voluntarily get in touch with the troopers like this? Kimmie had only talked to Meg that first day. Since Chuck refused to keep a landline and the tiny subdivision where they lived was notorious for its spotty cell coverage, she'd had to walk to the neighbor's and beg to borrow her phone for such a private conversation.

Taylor didn't deny that Meg had gotten involved. "At the scene ..." He stopped himself. "At your house, I mean, there were a few questions we had. And talking with your sister has raised even more."

Kimmie's brain was spinning but instead of an efficient machine taking her to the conclusions she needed to arrive at, the mental chaos was more like a hamster in a wheel, spinning helplessly but always remaining in the exact same spot.

"What kind of questions?" she found herself asking.

"Well, your sister says your mother wrote notes. Notes about how she felt at home." He leveled his gaze. "A few of the notes are at your sister's in Anchorage, but she thinks there's more. Can you think of any special place your mother may have kept them? A favorite hiding place? Somewhere private?"

Kimmie shook her head. The idea of privacy in a family like Chuck's was almost humorous.

Taylor sighed. "Well, if you think of something, will you let me know?"

"Sure." Kimmie stared at the wall.

Taylor waited until she looked straight at him. "Do you feel safe at home?"

Kimmie bristled. What happened in the privacy of Chuck's trailer was her business and no one else's. Nobody, not even an Alaska state trooper in his impeccably pressed uniform, had the right to pry into her life, unlocking all those secrets she vowed to keep buried and hidden.

She tilted up her chin. "Of course I do."

His eyes were full of empathy, and at that moment she wished she could escape his intense scrutiny.

"If you're sure. Some of the things your sister told us ..."

"Meg's Meg," Kimmie announced, as if that were all the explanation necessary. "She's dealing with her grief the only way she knows how. I'm just sorry it's causing more trouble and hassle for you at the station."

Taylor didn't look away as he reached into his breast pocket. "I want you to have my card," he said. "I'm writing my cell number on the back. You can call me any time. Call me at the station or at home if it's an emergency."

She had no idea just what kind of emergency she was expected to find herself in and certainly didn't feel like asking. She took the card, shoved it into her pocket, and vowed to forget about it. Forget Taylor and forget this nonsense about her mother's death. Meg was Meg, which might not mean anything to the trooper, but it meant a lot to her. Her sister was only out to raise trouble. That was all. Who knew what kind of lies she'd concocted about Kimmie and Pip and their life with Chuck? How would Meg even know? She hadn't been up to visit in years.

Taylor continued to stare at her intently, and she wished her mother hadn't raised her to be the kind of girl who was perfectly polite, perfectly unable to cut a conversation short because she didn't want to appear rude. She had no idea what this trooper was suspecting or insinuating, but she didn't have to sit here and take it. She could tell him to leave. It wasn't as if he owned the daycare.

But she continued to sit and stare, hoping he'd end the meeting on his own.

"I want you to think about what's best for your brother." What was he suggesting? Think about what was best for Pip? What else did Kimmie have to think about since their mother died? If she weren't thinking about what was best for Pip, she'd be in Anchorage by now, maybe even on her way to the Lower 48 if she found a way to get down there. A way to escape this chaos that had consumed her life.

Taylor had no idea what he was talking about.

"I really should get back to work now." Kimmie glanced up at an imaginary clock on the wall. "Thank you for your concern." Even now, she was unable to drop her upbringing, unable to be anything but polite and cordial.

Taylor reached out and touched her wrist. He didn't grab it, or she would have jerked away. The touch was shocking. Kimmie sat frozen for just a second.

"I just want to make sure you're safe, you and your brother both."

If Taylor was concerned for her safety like he claimed, he should have thought about that before talking about investigations prying into her private family affairs. If he wanted what was best for Pip, he'd stay far away from her home, from her stepfather.

Chuck hadn't been named as a suspect, but Kimmie was certain that if her sister were involved, Meg would have blamed Chuck. For years, Meg had begged Mom to leave Glennallen or at the very least to let Kimmie come live with her and her new husband in Anchorage. Finally, the fighting grew ugly enough that Chuck refused to let Mom have anything to do with her oldest daughter. It was just like Meg — spiteful, selfish Meg — to go around making accusations.

Not that they were entirely baseless. How many times had Chuck threatened to murder Kimmie's mom? How many times in a drunken rage had he beaten her so badly she passed out?

Kimmie's core was shaking when she walked the trooper to the door of the daycare, but it wasn't because she was mad at his suggestion Mom's death might not have been a suicide.

It was because he'd confirmed Kimmie's most secret fear, the one she'd been trying desperately to hide even from herself — that her stepfather could actually have committed the murder.

CHAPTER 12

Kimmie had a terrible headache and was grateful for Jade's help in getting the kids ready for their afternoon nap. Only a few of them fell asleep, but the rest managed to remain relatively quiet, looking at books or playing with a toy or two in their cots. Jade was getting ready to organize the bookshelves when Kimmie came behind her.

"Hey." She tried to keep her voice sounding as natural as possible.

Jade glanced up, and Kimmie rubbed her sweaty palms against her jeans. "Umm, do you still have free long distance on your cell?"

Jade pulled out her earbuds and yanked her phone out of her pocket. "Yeah. You need to call someone?"

All her co-workers at the daycare knew about Kimmie's phone situation, and whether or not they thought it was weird that a young woman living in the present day could survive without a cell phone or even a landline at her house, they always let her borrow their phones to make quick calls here and there.

Kimmie reached out for the cell, shuffling her feet and not quite able to meet Jade's gaze. "It might be a little longer than normal. I haven't really talked with any of the relatives since Mom died, and ..."

Jade waved her hand in the air. "Take it. Go. You can even head outside or something if you want privacy. We're fine here for a while."

Kimmie wasn't sure if she should be hurt by the way Jade was acting so dismissively or if she should simply be grateful for the chance to connect with someone outside Glennallen.

"I'll try not to be too long," she promised. Grabbing her coat, she made sure that Pip was comfortable in his cot. He was one of the only kids who regularly managed to drift off to sleep, and he was already drooling slightly when Kimmie made her way out to the playground. Sitting down on one of the swings, Kimmie dialed the number from memory, begging it to go through.

Please pick up. Please pick up.

Kimmie let out a simultaneous sigh of relief and a shiver from the cold. Swinging her legs softly back and forth, she found her voice.

"Hey, Meg. It's me, Kimmie. Got a minute? We need to talk about Mom."

CHAPTER 13

Kimmie waited so long for her sister's response she started to worry she'd called the wrong person. She pulled the phone away from her ear to check the number again.

"Meg?" she finally asked.

"I'm here." Her sister let out a sigh, and Kimmie braced herself for some sort of big-sister lecture or maybe a guilt trip. *Why didn't you know Mom was suicidal? Why didn't you do anything to stop her?*

Instead, Meg asked, "Are you okay? Where are you calling from? Is anyone else there?"

Kimmie knew she was talking about Chuck and shook her head even though her sister couldn't see the gesture. "No, it's just me. I'm at the daycare, but the kids are resting, so I'm on the playground. I'm by myself."

"Okay." Meg sounded relieved. "Listen, I'm really sorry I haven't gotten out there yet. I wanted to be with you. I really did."

It's not too late, Kimmie wanted to say, but her voice betrayed her, and she let out the expected, "It's okay. I know you're busy."

"It's not that." Meg sounded flustered, the same vibe she gave off to anyone and everyone. The vibe that yelled *I'm a busy woman with five hundred important things on my to-do list.* "I'm just worried for you. I don't want you staying with him, Kimmie."

Her heart sank. Why had she expected anything different? This wasn't a conversation between an older sister comforting her little sister, the same little sister who found their mother hanging from the garage rafters. This was a conversation where Meg simply continued the argument she'd started with Mom years ago, except now she was fighting with Kimmie: *Leave Chuck. Move in with me in Anchorage.*

"I can't leave Pip." If Meg had invested any time in getting to know her half-brother, she'd understand, but by the time Pip was born, she and Mom were in the ugliest stage of their *leave Chuck and let me save you* feud.

"Right now, it's you I'm worried about." Even while she spoke, Meg sounded like she had twenty other things on her mind, a hundred other errands she'd rather be doing than having this conversation with her disappointment of a sister.

That's easy for you to say from your privileged high tower, Kimmie wanted to shout. If her sister had stuck with the family instead of insisting on spending her senior year in Anchorage with that boyfriend who dumped her the week before prom and the best friend who gossiped about it behind her back, Meg would understand what things were really like under Chuck's roof.

Why Kimmie couldn't just walk away.

Why Mom couldn't either.

She tried to steady her voice. She wasn't Mom. This wasn't her fight to have with her sister. She just wanted information. "A trooper stopped by," she said, hoping that Meg would pick up the cue and fill her in on whatever details she'd given Taylor's station.

Silence.

"He said they're maybe going to look a little deeper into everything that happened." Kimmie waited. *Jump in at any time, Meg. Don't wait for me.*

Her sister let out an impatient huff. "Well, I'm worried about you, all right? There's some things you don't know. About Mom."

Kimmie rolled her eyes. So all of a sudden her sister was an expert on the dead mother she hardly visited? "Like what?" *This should be good*, Kimmie thought and waited for her sister's response.

"She called me last week."

That was news. "She did?" For the entirety of their relationship, at least as far as Kimmie knew, whenever Mom wanted to talk to her daughter she had to beg Chuck to let her go over to Mrs. Spencer's, the neighbor, to borrow the phone. Over the past few years he'd gotten so belligerent whenever Mom showed even a spark of independent thought, she simply stopped asking. Besides, weren't her mom and sister mad at each other since Meg always pestered Mom about leaving Chuck? From Meg's vantage point, Chuck was a jerk, and she couldn't understand why anyone would choose to stay in a relationship with someone that evil.

As if it were ever that simple.

"Listen, I don't have time to go into all the details right now." Meg lowered her voice as if she were worried about eavesdroppers. "But I want to talk to you soon. Can I come out there? I can shuffle some things around, drive out tomorrow ..."

She let her voice trail off. Kimmie tried to remember the last time she'd seen her sister. There had been one visit after Pip was born, which lasted long enough for Meg to drop off a few packages of diapers and two new onesies before she continued on her road trip to Denali with her husband and their cadre of rich, attractive friends. Then last December she pulled up in time to hand Mom a fruitcake and a pair of holiday socks before taking off toward the Fairbanks ice festival.

Apparently taking Kimmie's silence for reluctance or hostility, Meg added with a huff, "You know, it shouldn't take a death in the family to make us spend time together."

Kimmie wanted to remind Meg that she wasn't the one who left. It was Meg who stayed in Anchorage, Meg who abandoned her sister when she was arguably at her most vulnerable, leaving her and Mom to fend for themselves against Chuck's cruelty.

Kimmie recognized that her jealousy was misplaced. It wasn't like Meg could have done anything to assuage Chuck's anger. He would have been a terrible husband and a terrible stepparent and a terrible person whether or not Meg was there to share in the family's suffering. But the fact that Meg had gone on to attend college, found herself a successful husband to take her on so many exotic vacations, and was leading in every other way as functional and enviable a life as possible was an affront to Kimmie's sense of justice, immature and irrational as it might be.

Jade glanced out the door frowning, and Kimmie wondered just how long she'd been out here. It only felt like a few minutes, but of course a few minutes gave plenty of time to revive old grudges and poke at old scabs as far as her sister was concerned.

"Listen, Meg, I've got to hang up. I'm at work."

"Hold on. There's something I haven't told you." Meg was whining now, her voice rising in pitch. It was that same affected intonation that made her come across as cool and mature in high school but sounded grating and petty as an adult.

Jade was still staring at Kimmie, jerking her head now as if playing a game of charades, raising her eyebrows in some unspoken message. Goosebumps erupted at the base of Kimmie's neck, and she instinctively turned around. Her stepfather was just a foot behind her, glowering, his face somewhat droopy on account of all he'd had to drink.

"Just who d'you think you're talking to?" He grabbed Jade's cell phone. "Who're you?" he demanded coarsely, and Kimmie held her breath, straining to hear any response from the other line.

It was silent. Had Meg hung up?

All of Chuck's attention reverted back to Kimmie. "What're you doing with a cell phone? Didn't I tell you those things'll give you brain cancer?"

"It's not mine," Kimmie stammered. "I was just ..."

Jade rushed up, interrupting. "It was a prospective parent. A new family in town. They just had some questions about the daycare, and I was busy with the kids."

Kimmie felt her face heating up and didn't know if Jade's intervention made her feel more grateful or humiliated.

She winced when Chuck grabbed her arm, digging his dirt-crusted fingernails through her sweater. Dragging her away from Jade, he hissed, "Get the boy. You're coming home."

"It's not three yet," Kimmie protested. "I've got two more hours."

"Don't care," Chuck slurred. "And tell that big black gal you work with you quit. I can't find a single can of chili for lunch, and even if I did, I couldn't eat it because you lost the can opener. We're out of groceries, and the bathroom's a mess. You're coming home."

Kimmie didn't have the nerve to meet Jade's eyes but sensed her friend's gaze following her as she made her way into the daycare. Pip was still drooling on his cot, his hands tucked under his chin like a tiny cherub.

"Come on, Buster. Let's get you ready." She hated to wake him up. He looked so peaceful, and she knew he needed his sleep.

Pip stirred, and Kimmie smiled at him. "Wake up. It's time

to go home."

Back at the trailer, she'd confront Chuck. She had to. She and Pip needed this job just as much as Chuck needed the paycheck. He'd come around.

Kimmie wrapped Pip's arms around her neck so she could carry him to the cubbies to collect their things.

"You okay?" Jade whispered. Kimmie hadn't even noticed her trailing behind them.

She sniffed. "Yeah. He's just ... you know, still having a hard time. After everything." She wrapped Pip's coat around his shoulders and wondered if he was about to fall asleep again in her arms.

Jade looked unconvinced. "You need something? I can help, you know. I even have a spare bedroom if you and Pip need some time away for a little bit." She let the last part of her sentence inflect up to a question.

Kimmie squeezed back the anger and mortification that were boiling inside her. "That's really sweet of you. But we're fine." She rubbed her brother's back and looked Jade square in the eyes. "We're going to get through this. We always do."

CHAPTER 14

Back home, Kimmie helped Pip get situated in their room with the handful of matchbox cars Mom managed to buy for him at the thrift store. Once Kimmie was sure he was adequately distracted, she headed to the bathroom and started cleaning. Chuck must have had a bloody nose again. Splatters of red filled the sink. She looked inside the cabinet. Great, no gloves, either.

She grabbed a few paper towels and balled them together in as thick of a wad as she could, hoping the barrier was big enough to protect her from coming into contact with her stepfather's blood. Who knew what kind of diseases he might carry? Her stomach retched, and she remembered she hadn't eaten any lunch. Oh, well. At least Pip was fed. Whatever Jade heated up for the kids that afternoon might have to last him until tomorrow morning.

If Chuck let them go back to the daycare at all.

He couldn't really force her to quit her job. They needed

that money. Besides, he liked getting Pip out of the house. After three-day weekends when the daycare was closed for a holiday, Chuck would grumble and demanded to know when she would get that boy out of his hair.

A dozen times while she cleaned out the sink, Kimmie pictured herself walking into the living room, snapping off that stupid television set of his, and telling her stepfather he had no authority to make her leave her job. But then what? Even if he legally couldn't keep her from the daycare, he had every right to prevent Pip from going, and then what would be the point? She had to stay with Pip. She was his only protection from his father's violence. She would never leave the two of them at the trailer alone.

So if Chuck remained that stubborn about the daycare, if he said that he was withdrawing Pip from the program, did that mean she'd stay here, every bit a slave as her mom had been? The idea was unfathomable. She'd lose her mind. She'd go insane and kill herself like her mom had. Or kill her stepfather and wind up behind bars, with Pip imagining her a villain every bit as scary as the ones he saw on TV. No, she couldn't, she wouldn't stay here forever.

So what could she do?

She scrubbed at the sink fiercely until Chuck came in,

pushing past her with a grunt. He unzipped his pants and started to pee.

Disgusted, Kimmie threw down her paper towel, stomped into the hallway, and slammed the bathroom door shut. People shouldn't live like this. It was cruel and inhumane to subject a child as young and impressionable as Pip to this kind of squalor and filth.

Chuck cleared his throat from the bathroom, loudly enough that Kimmie could hear through the door and above the sound of the wailing TV. She didn't know what was on, but it certainly wasn't appropriate for children. Sometimes she wondered if Pip retreated into his own mind like he did because his surroundings were too difficult to accept.

No kid should have to endure what he had, but what could Kimmie do? How could she help him? She thought about Taylor. She'd had the trooper on her mind even before he showed up at her work today. Fingering his card in her pocket, she wondered if there was any way he could help her.

But how?

If Chuck wouldn't let Pip go back to the daycare, that meant she couldn't go back either. She couldn't abandon her brother that way. As far as she knew, Chuck had never physically hurt Pip, but he'd threatened to. It was one of his go-to responses whenever Kimmie or her mom showed any sign of rebellion. If Mom let the coffee run out, Chuck would tell her he was going to bash Pip's head against the wall. If Kimmie didn't sign over her entire daycare check to him, he'd threaten to starve Pip for the week. Who could guess what would happen to her brother if Kimmie defied Chuck's orders and went back to the daycare?

She'd have to find another way to convince him. She could bring up the money, but she'd already tried that. There had to be something else.

Chuck threw open the bathroom door, jostling her as he squeezed his wide girth down the hallway. Scratching at his hairy belly, he mumbled, "Outta my way," and plodded back toward his recliner.

Kimmie glanced at him in open disgust. Her mom had spent a decade with this man, subjecting Kimmie and later Pip to his barbaric ways, his explosive temper. And now Mom was gone, and there was no way Kimmie was going to waste the rest of her life cleaning up her stepfather's messes and rolling over to be his punching bag whenever a violent mood came over him.

She was going to get away from here, and she was taking her brother with her.

CHAPTER 15

By the time Kimmie got the bathroom at least relatively clean, Pip had fallen asleep, content to finish his interrupted nap at home. It was just as well. She was sure he needed the sleep. She still didn't know how he was processing their mother's death. He'd cried when the ambulance came to carry her body away, but how much did he really understand? Kimmie had tried to explain to him, but what words do you use to tell a three-year-old their mother is dead?

Chuck was taking an afternoon snooze in front of the TV, and Kimmie tiptoed into the kitchen and scanned the cupboards. It was one of her regular pastimes, something she liked to call *let's see how much food there is and figure out how many days we can make it last.*

Today she was lucky. She pulled down two cans of chili from the back of the cupboard and the heels leftover from Chuck's white bread. She could feed Pip dinner after all.

Glancing around at her sleeping stepfather, she wondered

how to make the best use of her time. If Pip were awake, she'd take him outside. It was chilly out, but the fresh air did both of them good. Every winter brought two or three major cases of sinus infections, and Chuck refused to let anyone see the doctor. The family could easily qualify for state insurance, but Chuck claimed the application process invaded their privacy and was convinced that Alaskan doctors were paid off for killing the most Medicaid recipients.

Kimmie hated feeling so helpless, and just a few months ago at work she'd printed and filled out the forms to get Pip onto Alaska's free health care for children. She used the daycare's address instead of their own and figured she'd keep the card there too in case Pip ever needed it, but the system was so backed up it would still be several months before she'd receive any kind of answer.

And Kimmie didn't plan to stay here that long.

All afternoon while she cleaned, she'd been thinking through her conversation with Taylor, running through each fact and insinuation.

Mom didn't write a suicide note. Or if she did, nobody had found it yet. If Mom wanted people to read that note, she would have left it somewhere obvious. Kimmie had no idea how many suicide victims really did write letters for their families to find, but the trooper thought it was strange enough to at least mention its absence.

Mom had been in contact with Meg. About what? Chuck had sneaked up behind her while she was talking to her sister, interrupting their call before Kimmie could find anything else out. So what had Mom and Meg been talking about? How had Mom even reached out to Meg without Chuck finding out?

Meg didn't think Mom killed herself. Did Taylor actually say those words, or was that just the meaning Kimmie pieced together on her own? Meg had contacted the troopers. The troopers were investigating the case. Therefore, Meg must have given them some sort of information that cast suspicion on the suicide theory.

Meg didn't think Kimmie was safe. Meg asked her again to come to Anchorage, only this time it wasn't so she could sweep in and save the day and set herself up as Kimmie's parent-replacement, bossing her around and nagging her for all the ways she didn't live up to Meg's expectations. At least it didn't feel that way.

Not this time.

Meg wanted Kimmie to leave Chuck. That was nothing new. She'd wanted Kimmie to leave as soon as she knew or at least suspected what kind of man their stepfather was. There was nothing legally preventing Kimmie from leaving, and even though Chuck would be mad to lose a free source of domestic labor, he was too lazy to come all the way down to Anchorage to cause her any problems.

She could walk away now and never look back.

But what would happen to Pip? Relentlessly, her mind replayed the dozens of times Chuck had used Pip as a hostage to force Kimmie or her mom to do what he wanted. She could pass that information on to Taylor, but would anything happen? What if Taylor came back and said that he couldn't take any action unless she could prove Chuck actually harmed Pip? She was stuck.

But she wouldn't stay that way forever. There was some way out of this maddening prison. There had to be.

She just wished she knew what it was.

CHAPTER 16

Pip woke up from his nap crying. No, that wasn't the right word for it. Shrieking.

Kimmie had never heard any human make sounds like that, not in her entire life. She'd been heating up the last of the chili to get ready for dinner when she heard the shrill screams. Running to Pip's room, she braced herself for something terrible. His clothes were engulfed in flames. Chuck was stabbing him with the knife he'd used to butcher moose back in the days before he grew too lazy to go hunting.

But no. Chuck wasn't there, and as Kimmie knelt on the floor by the mattress, she couldn't see anything wrong. "What is it, Buster?" she asked, but Pip only continued to scream as if his intestines had caught fire. She examined his body, looking for injury, trying to guess where he hurt. Could it be his appendix or something else internal that she couldn't see? She had to get him to medical care, but how?

"Pip? Where do you hurt, Buster?"

He thrashed from side to side. She had to calm his movements. If she could just make eye contact, she could try to communicate. She curled him up on her lap, doing what she could to hold his head still so he wouldn't hurt himself with his wild flailing. When she saw the look in his eyes, her words caught in her throat. That wasn't her brother. It was someone else. Something else. His eyes were entirely vacant, reminding her mercilessly of her mother's corpse.

He stared at her, still unseeing, and shrieked again.

Terrified, she hefted him into her arms and raced him into the living room. "Something's wrong." She didn't care how worried Chuck was about money. She didn't care how much he hated the idea of doctors treating welfare patients. Pip needed medical attention. Now.

Chuck blinked at his son, and for a moment his face blanched. Kimmie didn't know if she should be grateful that he was taking Pip's condition seriously or if his reaction only freaked her out more.

"He woke up screaming," she explained, panting. "I don't know what to do." Her heart was racing, both from the physical energy it spent to keep her brother from flinging himself out of her arms and from her fear for his safety.

Chuck looked as bewildered as she felt, so she dared to

squeak, "Should I take him to the doctor?"

The words seemed to snap Chuck out of his fearful reverie his son's behavior had cast him into. He scowled. "No." He stood up from the recliner, toppling Pringles crumbs and a crushed beer can onto the carpet.

He took a step forward and stared at his son. "Night terrors," he announced factually. "You've just got to wake him up."

Kimmie forced herself to look at those expressionless eyes again. "But he is awake. See?"

Chuck shook his head. "No, he ain't." He raised his fist in the air, and before Kimmie could react, he brought it down onto her brother's belly. Pip opened his mouth like a fish trying to gulp air, and in an instant the blank, glossy eyes took on an expression of fear and pain. He sucked in a noisy inhale then started to cry

"See?" Chuck turned back around and lumbered to his seat. "All you gotta do is wake him up."

Kimmie turned her back and hurried with Pip into the bedroom. She fingered the card in her pocket, where Taylor had written out his number, telling her to call if she ever needed help.

Through his tears, Pip clung onto Kimmie's shoulders but no longer flailed around or acted possessed. Kimmie took in a choppy inhalation and sank down with him on the mattress. Stroking his sweat-drenched hair, she fingered Taylor's card with her other hand and promised her brother, "I'm going to find us a way out of here. I'm going to get us some help."

CHAPTER 17

Dinner had been doomed from the start. During the entire time Kimmie was dealing with Pip and his night terrors, she'd left the chili on the stove. By the time she realized her mistake, half of the meal had turned into black crisp.

She would have never served it to her stepdad, but that was the last of the chili, so she added a few prayers and half a can of water, hoping to mask the burnt taste and stretch the meager offering out as much as possible. She scooped the top portion, the part that was the least scalded, into a bowl for Chuck and split the rest between herself and Pip. Even though Chuck never ate the heels of his bread, Kimmie couldn't serve the portions to Pip at the table without infuriating her stepfather, so she slipped them beneath her sweater to store for later.

Pip would sleep better with a snack before bed, anyway.

"This tastes awful," Chuck declared after his first bite. "What'd you do to it?"

Kimmie caught Pip's eyes on her. For her brother's sake,

she'd try to avoid a confrontation. It would take every ounce of her patience and self-possession, but to keep Pip safe, it was worth the effort.

"I'm sorry." Kimmie eyed her own bowl, which contained nothing but black tar and a few beans. "It got a little burned."

Chuck spat, his saliva landing on the edge of the table instead of the floor where he probably intended. "What kind of stupid idiot can't even cook chili?"

She poked at the lumps in her bowl and offered another apology, one she mentally promised herself would be her last. She had to stop this, stop groveling. Mom had done nothing but cower before Chuck, and look where it had gotten her. For years, Kimmie had been plagued with both the urge to protect her mother and the unbearable frustration of knowing Mom was too weak to leave. Kimmie hated the way Mom refused to stand up to Chuck, the way she let him beat her up without offering up even the faintest of protests.

For years, Kimmie simultaneously despised, feared for, and pleaded with her mom, also vowing to herself that she would never let another man ruin her life the way Chuck had ruined her mother's. But now look where she was. It hadn't even been a full week since Mom's death, and Kimmie was falling into the exact same passive role, submissively trying to placate her stepfather because she was too scared to see Pip hurt.

It gave her an entirely new outlook on what Mom had experienced the last ten years of her life. What if the reason she stayed with Chuck wasn't because she was too weak to leave him but because she was scared of what he might do to her kids? By the time Pip came around, she must have felt even more trapped. For years, Kimmie wondered why her mom hadn't simply walked away, had cried herself to sleep at night asking God why her mom hated her and Pip enough to keep them trapped here.

Maybe Kimmie had been wrong. Maybe it was her love for her children that bound her mother to this monster.

Kimmie had vowed to never repeat the same mistakes her mom did, but wasn't she doing the exact same thing? Apologizing to Chuck because she didn't want him to get angry and possibly hurt her brother. Persevering in this purgatory of an existence because her only other option was to leave Pip alone with his father, abandoning the brother she loved.

"Why aren't you eating that, boy?"

Kimmie's spine stiffened while Chuck glared at Pip's bowl of burnt chili. Pip glanced to her, and she rushed to fill the silence. "They had a pretty big lunch this afternoon at work." Wrong thing to say. Why did she mention the daycare?

Chuck grabbed his son's bowl and shoved it under his chin. "You eat this food your sister made, or you're gonna be sleeping outside with the bears and the moose tonight."

Pip's eyes widened.

Chuck sneered, taking apparent pleasure in his son's fear. "That's right. Pretend like you understand what I'm saying. Pretend like you're not some stupid, idiotic ..."

Kimmie was clutching the sides of her chair to keep from jumping up and slapping him. Tears stung the corners of her eyes, not of anger or fear or even grief, but of sheer hatred. She wanted to see Chuck dead. She wanted to be there when he gasped his last breath, his ugly, gaping mouth hanging open, his curses finally silenced. The hatred coursed through her entire body, fueling her. She began to shake. The only thing that kept her from seizing whatever utensil she could grab hold of and attacking her stepfather was that she didn't want to scare her brother.

"Eat your chili, Buster," she whispered.

"That's right," Chuck mocked in an imitating falsetto. *"Eat your chili, Buster*, because you're lucky I even let you sit at my table. You know what most parents do to little boys who don't know how to talk by the time they're your age? They make them crawl on the floor and lick up their food like dogs." He jabbed his spoon toward his son. "That's what I'm gonna do with you if you don't eat every single bite from your bowl, you hear me?"

Kimmie turned toward her brother and scooped a small spoonful of chili into his mouth. Trying to shut out the sound of Chuck jeering at his son for having to be fed like an infant, she pictured a life free from everything. Free from Chuck, free from this revolting trailer. Free from her grief and her guilt, free from the questions about her mom's death that plagued her.

"That's right," Chuck taunted, his voice rising in pitch. "Feed the tiny little baby. Then don't forget to change his diaper too. Is your diaper dirty, you stupid little idiot?"

Kimmie kept her back to him. He was egging her on, a dinner game he'd played hundreds of times with her mother. Teasing and jeering until Mom started to cry or showed some other display of emotion, enough to fuel Chuck's sadism until he felt he had the right to heap physical abuse on top of the verbal. Kimmie refused to fall victim in this game of his. She wasn't going to give him the privilege of seeing her emotions, of sensing her fear. She wasn't going to show any sign of weakness.

He could beat her if he wanted, but her mind and soul belonged to her alone. She wondered what he'd do if he realized how much hatred she hid buried beneath her expressionless exterior, how many times she'd sat at this same table and visualized his pained and tortured death.

No, it wasn't a Christian attitude. Mom had taught her to forgive anyone who wronged her, but Mom wasn't here anymore, and her strategy of rolling over like a compliant dog welcoming its master's boot wasn't going to get Kimmie anything but injured. She knew that the Bible talked about love and grace and forgiveness, but there were also times for wrath.

And right now, the thing she prayed for most was for God to afflict her stepfather with every kind of disease and painful torment in his vast, almighty repertoire.

The thought fueled her determination, and she fed her brother in silence.

CHAPTER 18

It was Kimmie's good luck that the electric company decided to make good on their threat to cut off the power that night in response to a delinquent bill. Chuck's plot of land, like many others in the area, came equipped with a wooden outhouse, a remnant from Alaska's homesteading days, and as she led her brother outside, she had the chance to speak to him in private.

"The way your dad's treating us isn't right." She'd lost track of how many nights after a dinner just like this, or worse, her mom would hold Pip in her arms and croon, "Your father loves you. He just doesn't always know how to show it," or some other nonsense. Kimmie figured Pip was confused enough by his father's abuse that he didn't need anyone else making excuses for such unforgivable behavior.

"I'm trying to think of a way to get us to a safe place. Would you like that?" She searched her brother's face for any sign that he heard or understood.

88

"It's not always going to be like this. We can pray ..." She stopped herself. What was she trying to tell him? That they could pray and God would whisk them to safety as if he were a genie from a magic lamp? How many sleepless nights had Kimmie spent after moving in with Chuck, begging God to free her from that existence? To strike her new stepfather dead or make Mom brave enough to leave him or do something to stop the torture she constantly lived through.

But God hadn't answered her prayers. Ten years later, he still hadn't answered. She was still here, an adult but every bit as much dependent on her stepfather as she'd been in her teens. She wasn't mad at God, but she didn't want Pip to end up doing what she did, setting all her hopes on a prayer, a prayer that failed to come true. Kimmie still talked to God, but mostly it was to ask him to shield Pip from the worst of the horrors they had learned to endure.

She didn't have the strength to hope for anything more.

Mom was different. Mom had kept her faith until the very end. "God's got a reason for everything," she'd say while icing Kimmie's black eye so the bruise wouldn't raise quite as many questions at school. "We can always trust God to do what's best for us in any situation." That was another one of her favorites.

Kimmie didn't doubt God's goodness. She'd experienced

waves of peace that swept over her during the depths of her turmoil and inner pain, signs of God's love she knew were divine. What she did doubt was her mom's simplistic expectation that if they remained steadfast and patient, God would usher them into some happily-ever-after dream world where Chuck was kind and their dilapidated, drafty trailer transformed itself into a home like her sister Meg's mansion on the Anchorage hillside.

If Kimmie wanted the fairy tale ending, she'd have to find a way to work out the details on her own. Sitting around waiting patiently had gotten her mom killed — yet another mistake Kimmie was in no hurry to repeat. She felt Taylor's card in her pocket, gleaning vicarious strength and courage. Just knowing someone else cared about her safety, someone with the authority of the state backing him up, gave her an unfamiliar sense of boldness and determination.

She would find a way. She would break free from this cage. She would find her happy ending, and she would give Pip the life he deserved.

Kimmie fingered Taylor's card. The outhouse was situated halfway between Chuck's trailer and their nearest neighbor. Mrs. Spencer was an elderly woman who sometimes let Kimmie use her phone. If she left Pip here and started to run ...

She glanced at her brother, who sat on the outhouse toilet. No, not yet. The last thing she needed was for Pip to follow her and slow her down or fall down the outhouse hole if she left him here alone. Her plan would have to wait. Tonight. Not so late that Mrs. Spencer would be in bed or alarmed by a knock on her door, but late enough that Pip would hopefully be asleep and Kimmie could come out here alone.

Thank God they'd cut off the power.

Her mind made up, she helped Pip off the seat and cleaned him up. Without any running water at home and nothing stored in bottles, they'd skip brushing their teeth tonight. You couldn't get a cavity from one act of negligence.

She held Pip's hand and shuddered as they made their way back to the trailer. An icy blast stabbed through her sweater. The sun was setting earlier and earlier each day, a sign of winter's soon arrival just as telling and ominous as the termination dust on the mountains. She wasn't going to spend another winter here in a trailer that could never heat up past fifty-five degrees, power that turned on and off based on when Chuck remembered to pay his overdue bills. By the time the winter solstice came, when it was dark by three and the sun refused to rise until after ten, she wasn't going to dig around for candle nubs because Chuck drank away their utility money.

She was going to be in a warm home by a roaring fireplace, making as much hot chocolate as she and Pip could ever care to drink, both of them tucked up in blankets and relaxing on the softest couch imaginable. She'd take Pip to the library, check out an endless supply of books, and read them all to him for hours at a time. Of course, she'd save her best voices for when it was just the two of them together.

They would be happy.

And they would be safe.

She gave her brother's hand a squeeze. "Come on, Buster. Let's get you home."

CHAPTER 19

Kimmie hoped that with the electricity cut off, Chuck would fall asleep early. Without his TV to keep him company, there wasn't much else for him to do. It was far too much to expect him to get up and attack that pile of dirty dishes in the kitchen, and besides, without the electricity the well didn't run. In the early days after Mom moved in with Chuck, the trailer was hooked up to a generator to prepare for Glennallen's sporadic power outages, but it had fallen into disrepair, and Chuck always maintained it was too expensive to fix.

Kimmie was looking forward to a quiet night. Chuck couldn't expect her to stay up and clean, not with the sun down and no running water. She might crawl in bed with Pip and cuddle for a while until it was time for her to go back out. She wasn't exactly sure what she'd do if she managed to make use of Mrs. Spencer's phone, but maybe the extra couple hours would give her time to think up a plan.

Back inside the trailer, she helped Pip take off his coat.

Chuck was in his chair, waiting for her. "Put the kid to bed then come out here."

She didn't know what he wanted, but at least Pip would be excused from whatever sadism Chuck might have in mind. It was the most Kimmie could ask for, at least at the moment. In a few hours, she'd tell Chuck she had to use the outhouse and head over to the neighbor's. Mrs. Spencer usually turned off her lights around nine, so Kimmie would plan her visit shortly before that. She'd call Taylor.

And then what?

The seed of a plan had started to germinate in her mind, but it would take time to fully form. She had to muse over it for a little while. It couldn't be rushed. Whatever Chuck needed her for, she hoped it wouldn't take too long. She helped Pip into his favorite pajamas, teaching him the names of the dinosaurs — at least the ones she could remember — while pointing to the pictures. Sometimes she wondered if any of her extra effort to coax Pip to talk was getting through, but she'd never stop. She was convinced that Pip had more to say, more to learn, more to achieve than those who just knew him as a speech-delayed child would ever give him credit for. With Mom dead, Kimmie was now her brother's only champion and advocate.

She knew she certainly wasn't ready for the challenge, but it had been thrust upon her nonetheless.

"God will always equip you to do the work he's called you to do," Mom used to say, but at the time Kimmie had been more worried about keeping her stepfather from knocking her out than she'd been about growing in her faith. Still, Mom continued to sprinkle these little devotional moments into their days, teaching her about the Lord and his plan of salvation. The spiritual upbringing in the family was now another task that rested entirely on Kimmie's shoulders. Had she ever talked to Pip about heaven and sin and forgiveness? She wouldn't know how to have a conversation like that with a neurotypical three-year-old. What was she supposed to say to Pip?

All that would have to wait. The longer she tarried in the bedroom, the angrier and more impatient Chuck would grow. She kissed Pip's cheek, but he struggled and clung to her when she tried to tuck him in.

"What's wrong?" she asked. "What do you need?"

He made a back and forth motion with his fingers near his mouth. The pantomime was easy to discern. "You want to brush your teeth?"

He responded with a grunt.

"There's no water tonight. It's okay. It won't be too bad to skip it for just this once."

Pip's eyes widened as if Kimmie had just confessed that she was the one who killed their mom, and she let out her breath. "Fine," she breathed, "just stay here for a little bit, and if you're still awake when I come back, we'll brush your teeth then."

She had no idea how she'd manage that without any tap or running water, but she'd figure something out. Prying herself free from his hold, she blew him a kiss and hurried to the door.

She'd kept her stepfather waiting long enough.

CHAPTER 20

Chuck was cleaning out his ears when Kimmie stepped back into the living room.

"You wanted to see me?"

He didn't turn to look at her. "Got these for you." He tossed a manila envelope by her feet. "Need them filled out by tomorrow when the mail comes."

She picked up the envelope as well as a few of Chuck's used Q-tips. "What's this?" She bent back the fastener.

"Disability application. You'll need that now you aren't working no more."

Kimmie's mom had never been one to gamble. She thought cards and dice were wicked, and she never took any risks. Kimmie wasn't like that, so she searched Chuck's face to try to detect how serious he was. This might all be some bluff. She could put up a tiny fight and be back at the daycare by tomorrow.

Or Chuck might be so set on keeping Kimmie at home that

he'd do anything, even hurt Pip, if she defied his order.

Just how far should she push? And was she feeling lucky?

Like earlier, she decided to appeal to his greed and selfishness first. "You know, I think the state's really backed up right now on applications." She wouldn't mention her own firsthand experience applying for Pip's medical coverage. "It'd probably take a while for the money to start coming through." She also wouldn't mention the fact that no reasonable administration would label her unfit for work. Because Chuck had managed to eke money out of the system for years for no other disability than being a lazy alcoholic who preferred his drink over gainful employment, that didn't mean that anyone who filled out this packet could count on receiving a regular check.

Filling out his stupid application would get him off her back, but it wouldn't put breakfast in Pip's mouth.

"Another thing I started to wonder just now," she began, trying like usual to downplay her ability to actively think and reason for herself, "is if maybe we'd be better off in the long run keeping things the way they are." She didn't say the word *daycare*, didn't want to trigger him and set him off for a half-hour tirade. She could tell by the tightness in his face that she was walking on thin ice, but she'd have to venture out just a little further and hope it wouldn't crack.

"The nice thing about the current setup is it has Pip eating most of his meals outside of the home. It'd take quite a bit more grocery money to make up that difference." She watched Chuck warily, knew that he was still unconvinced. "He's usually really hungry by bedtime," she added hopefully.

It was this last comment that tipped the scale against her.

"You think I'm not doing my job as the man of this house in providing for my family?" His diction for once was impeccable, which only increased Kimmie's fear. Her stepfather was mean, violent, and sadistic whenever he was drunk, but he tired easily and soon lost interest.

When he was sober, on the other hand ...

"I didn't mean that at all." She opened the envelope and pretended to look through the first few pages. "I'm sorry. It's just, things have been a little difficult for us all ..."

"Difficult?" her stepdad roared. "You want to talk to me about difficult? Your mom had the nerve to hang herself in my garage, leaving me an idiot of a son who can't even say his own name and an ungrateful brat who stands in my house and tells me how to run my family!"

Kimmie shook her head vehemently. "I'm sorry. That's not what I meant."

He was out of his chair now, and Kimmie didn't know whether the first object to meet her body would be his fists, his boots, or some projectile. He grabbed her by the ponytail, snapping her neck back and twisting her head up to face him.

"Let's get one thing right, you spoiled little princess," he hissed into her face. For once, she wished for the familiar scent of beer on his breath. "This is my home, and as long as you live here, you better expect we're going to do things my way. If I say go on disability, you go on disability. If I say punch your brother for being a stupid, speechless idiot, you punch your brother for being a stupid, speechless idiot."

All day, Kimmie had been testing this thought in her head, this nagging suspicion Taylor had fueled with his speculations and questions back at the daycare. Was this the kind of outrage Mom witnessed before her husband killed her? Kimmie was smart enough to know that she was stupid not to feel scared. Stupid not to cower, to get on her knees, to beg for forgiveness.

But she wasn't ever going to grovel again. For the first time in her life, she saw her stepfather for what he really was — a pathetic, lonely man with no power except what people like her mom gave him. Mom fed his ego, bolstered his twisted sadism. If Chuck didn't have someone weaker to manipulate and terrify, he was absolutely nothing more than a potbellied man, a pathetic creature unable to wield any power whatsoever.

For the first time since she met Chuck, Kimmie wasn't scared of him. He could do what he wanted to her, then when he was done, he'd fall down exhausted and have to sleep until morning. She was younger, stronger, and more stubborn than he could ever hope to be. She was smarter too, which meant that she'd find a way to save both herself and Pip.

The torment would end, and Chuck would be left alone in a drafty, cold trailer, surrounded by beer cans and chip wrappers, with nobody left to terrorize, berate, or clean up after his pitiful messes.

Kimmie grinned.

And then realized from the glowing hatred in her stepfather's eyes that this single gesture of defiance might cost her very life.

CHAPTER 21

"You think this is a game?" Chuck punched Kimmie in the gut, his breath hot as he bellowed in her face. "You think you can come here and laugh at me in my own house?"

The anger that soared through her was as exhilarating as it was dangerous. Struggling for breath, she knew she couldn't irritate him further. She had to placate him. For Pip's sake.

But all she could think about was how pathetic he'd look in an orange prison jumpsuit, tired and weary, an old man who'd destroyed everyone around him and was finally reaping the benefits of his cruelty.

He slammed her against the wall and laughed as she collapsed to the floor. It wasn't until he unlocked his cabinet in the corner that cold fear chilled her whole body. He'd threatened each of them before with his rifle, even Pip, but that was always when he was so drunk he could hardly stand up straight.

She'd never faced him both armed and sober. All feelings of

haughtiness and grandeur vaporized when he pulled out his hunting rifle. That's what he called it at least, because apparently before he found a woman he could send to the grocery store to buy canned chili, he actually had to work for his food. Kimmie was still on the floor, wondering if she'd have time to kick him and knock him off balance if he decided he was going to fire.

Please don't let Pip come out, she prayed and hoped that her brother was already asleep.

Chuck took a step forward. She'd already missed the opportunity to trip him with her leg. She was paralyzed, watching every one of her stepfather's movements as though through time-manipulating binoculars. Chuck himself was stuck in slow motion as he brought the rifle up to his shoulder and aimed, but everything else — her pulse, her eyes darting in every direction in search of escape, her choppy breaths — had sped up exponentially.

Chuck slid the bolt forward. He was going to shoot her. Right here as she lay cowering on the floor, he was going to shoot her. She didn't even have the courage to bring her hands to cover her face but instead stared at her stepfather, totally stupefied.

A defiant whine from the hallway was both grating and

freeing. Kimmie jumped into action and sped toward her brother.

"Get him out of here," Chuck hollered.

Pip squealed angrily, pantomiming a toothbrush with his finger.

"He wants to brush his teeth."

"Just get him back in bed." At least Chuck had the decency to wait to murder Kimmie until Pip was safe in his room.

Heart still speeding, Kimmie led her brother down the hall. The electricity had been cut off so many times she always kept a small flashlight in the top drawer of the bathroom. She turned it on, wondering how to help Pip clean his teeth without any running water.

"Here. Open your mouth." She picked up his toothbrush, and he grunted in complaint, pointing to the tube of Colgate.

"No toothpaste," she told him, "not tonight. Now open up."

As she brushed his teeth, she brought her mouth toward his ear. "I want you to listen to me. No matter what you hear happening tonight, I want you to stay in your room, okay? If Daddy gets real loud, just stay in your room, and if he comes in acting mad ..."

She couldn't finish. What could she tell him? She wasn't even sure if Pip understood anything she said. If something happened to her and then Chuck came after Pip ... He could run. He knew where Mrs. Spencer lived. But what if he got lost in the dark?

"If Daddy's really mad tonight," she concluded, "it's okay to hide. You remember hide and seek at the daycare?" The thought gave her an idea. "Remember how you hid in that big house?"

Pip's eyes widened. Did he understand? She leaned in even closer. "If Daddy gets really mad and if I fall asleep or can't help you, I want you to hide. And if the sun comes out and you can sneak outside real quiet, go over to Mrs. Spencer. Can you do that?"

Wait. What if Mrs. Spencer just walked him back home to Chuck? It was too complicated. If Kimmie wasn't there to offer him every single direction like she'd spoon-fed him that night's chili for dinner, how could she expect Pip to remember everything?

Which meant that Kimmie had to keep herself alive through the night so that tomorrow she could find a way to get them both the help they needed.

By the time she got Pip tucked back into his bed, Chuck was back in his recliner. She glanced nervously around the living room until her eyes landed on the rifle leaning against the cabinet.

"Don't forget your application." Chuck nodded toward the pile of paperwork Kimmie had dropped on the floor.

If it helped her survive to see Pip through one more night, she'd go through the motions of obedience. Kimmie stooped to pick the file up and glanced again at the cabinet, promising herself that as soon as Chuck was asleep, she'd find a way to get a hold of that rifle.

CHAPTER 22

The temperature had dropped, but the sun still hadn't fully set. Another month or two and it would be dark before dinnertime, but for now the little bit of extra daylight still served in her favor. Pip had been snoring gently for about half an hour, and Kimmie's eyes were strained from filling out that paperwork with nothing but the dim twilight and a cheap battery-powered flashlight.

When she heard the front door shut, she strained her eyes and peered out the window. When Chuck had to pee and the power was out, he either filled up the toilet or sprayed the area right by the front porch, but this time she could make out his fat figure sauntering toward the outhouse.

Her whole body trembled. She'd already planned what she was going to do, but what if Chuck found out? What if they ran out of time? Then what would happen to them?

Before grabbing Pip, she ran to the gun cabinet. Chuck still hadn't put the rifle away. She'd never even handled the thing. Guns scared her, whether she was watching her stepfather aiming the barrel at her mom's chest or just seeing a gunfight on one of his violent TV shows. But this was the only way to make her plan work. She was faster than Chuck, but she certainly wasn't faster than a bullet.

She sprinted back into her room, trying to guess how long she had, begging God that it would be enough. Sometimes Chuck only needed a few minutes. Other times he could take nearly half an hour, although that was usually when he was in the house and had magazines to keep him busy.

She scooped Pip up, hoping he'd stay asleep until they were out of earshot. He'd be groggy and disoriented, and the last thing she needed was for Chuck to hear Pip crying as they made their escape. The biggest difficulty would be how to carry her brother and the rifle at the same time. She could just hide it. That way if Chuck went after them, at least he'd be unarmed. She didn't have a lot of time to make her decision. Instead of taking it with her and risking falling and hurting herself or her brother, she rushed it into their bedroom and shoved it under her mattress. All she needed was a few minutes' head start. She couldn't take Pip to Mrs. Spencer's. That would be too obvious and one of the first places Chuck would look. They'd have to go in the other direction. Kimmie needed to end up at the highway if she wanted to find someone with a phone who could help, but her main priority would be to evade Chuck for as long as possible. That was the first goal. Everything else was secondary.

Kimmie yanked their blanket off the bed and covered her brother. Tattered as it was, it'd give Pip some extra protection from the cold. Thankful that he was still asleep, she hurried as quickly as she could toward the front door, grabbing her jacket. Where were her shoes? There wasn't any more time to waste. She threw them on her feet, snatched up her brother's tennies, and was out the door.

Chuck hadn't been hunting in over ten years, but Kimmie didn't know just how good of a sportsman he'd been in the past. Could he follow their tracks? Would he bother in this chilly twilight? She'd need to make her way to the trooper station, but first the long trek through the woods, away from the highway, away from the neighbors who might offer to help.

As soon as she stepped outside, she wished she'd brought that rifle. She wasn't even positive that she'd know how to fire it if she needed to, but at least she'd look imposing. Then again, she couldn't carry her brother and an awkward gun very far. Pip was getting heavy. The woods thickened just ahead. Once she was convinced they were concealed by the trees and the darkness, she'd wake him up.

She hoped she hadn't forgotten anything.

Going back was no longer an option. No second chances, no second guessing.

She had to go forward.

Even if it killed her.

CHAPTER 23

Pip woke up when a branch pulled back and slapped his shoulder. Kimmie was panting. She hadn't realized how tired she'd get carrying him for even this short distance. Wrapping the blanket more tightly around his shoulders, she leaned against a tree trunk and cuddled him close to her chest.

"It's okay, Buster," she said. "We're going to go on a little ..." A little what? What kind of name could she give to a situation like this?

"We're going on a trip," she finally explained. "And I want you to be strong and brave, all right? Can you do that for me?"

Pip was looking around at the trees in all directions. His eyes widened, and he clutched Kimmie's coat.

"It's okay," she crooned as calmly as she could. "I know just where we're going, and I'm going to stay with you." She wanted to promise that he was safe now, but how could she be sure it was the truth? Instead, she bit her tongue and started to sing one of Mom's Bible verse songs.

Thy word is a lamp unto my feet and a light unto my path.

It seemed appropriate for a night like this, when the deepening woods grew more and more menacing as twilight faded into darkness. Kimmie never had a great sense of direction, but without landmarks to guide her and only the light from the moon and stars, she felt even more lost. There was the big dipper, a staple in the Alaskan sky. If she followed it to Polaris, she was supposed to be able to find north, but the entire constellation tipped on its side and loomed so low on the horizon it hardly looked like it was pointing anywhere. And even if she knew were north was, that didn't tell her which direction the trooper station was from here.

The farther she got from her neighbors or the Glenn Highway, the more lost she and Pip could get, but what other choice did she have? If Chuck hadn't found out she was missing yet, he would any minute. Unless he was so tired he went right to his recliner after using the outhouse and fell asleep. It was possible. She doubted he was in the habit of spying on her and Pip at night to make sure they were both in their room.

Unless Chuck had a reason to suspect otherwise, wouldn't he just assume they were asleep? Then she'd have until morning to find her and Pip the help they needed. Taylor and the other troopers would offer their protection as soon as she told them about the way her stepfather had threatened her with his rifle.

The rifle. Why had she moved it? Chuck would notice it wasn't there. She should have left it totally alone. She and Pip could have been safe.

"Come on, Buster." She slipped on Pip's tennis shoes and tried to figure out the best way to keep him wrapped in the blanket without having him constantly tripping over the edges. "Look," she said after she wrapped it up. "It's a cape. You're like a superhero now."

Pip still looked as if he were on the verge of a meltdown. She needed help. Didn't God understand she couldn't do this if Pip was screaming and throwing a fit? Not that she could blame him. She was terrified, but she at least had the privilege of understanding why they were out here in the cold and dark. Pip must feel completely lost and clueless. She gave him one last hug before urging him on.

"Let's go, Buster. We've got to walk a ways, but you're big and strong and brave, right?" Even as she said the words, Kimmie wished she could feel any of those things at the moment.

A cold wind blew, and she cursed her thin jacket. At least Pip looked warm wrapped up in his blanket. She just hoped he'd be able to walk without tripping. She'd carry him farther if she had to, but right now all her energy was focused on keeping herself from hyperventilating from fear. She hummed a few lines from her mom's Bible verse song, coaxed Pip forward, and they were on their way.

ALANA TERRY

CHAPTER 24

Kimmie couldn't believe it actually worked. She wasn't great with gauging time, but she figured it must have been close to an hour by now since they left Chuck's trailer. And so far, no angry yells or terrifying rifle blasts had pursued her and her brother.

She and Pip were deep in the woods now, but she'd followed a trail that was relatively straight. If she turned left and then circled back, she'd end up somewhere along the Glenn. Once she reached the highway, she'd be able to figure out where they were, and it was just a matter of time before they'd be safe at the trooper's station. In a way, she was grateful Chuck had pulled the rifle on her earlier in the evening. It gave her solid evidence she could pass on to Taylor and the others. Surely they'd agree with her that a three-year-old shouldn't be kept in a home with a father that volatile. She and Pip would finally be safe.

They would finally be free.

She continued to sing her Mom's little songs. Pip would whine restlessly if she grew quiet, and if she were being honest with herself, the Bible verses calmed her down too. Her body was shivering from cold, but she warmed herself with thoughts of a future safe with Pip. They'd move to Anchorage. Life wouldn't be a fairy tale squatting in Meg's home, but hopefully that situation would only be temporary. There must be daycares in town that needed a full-time worker and had room to enroll one more preschooler. It might not be the easiest way to make a living, but just about anything was better than staying in Glennallen with Chuck.

And no more canned chili for dinner.

Ever.

She could take Pip to church. Chuck thought all religion was nonsense and refused to let his family attend any services, but now that they were free, Kimmie could find a church in Anchorage with a good children's program where her brother could learn about the Lord. Even though she remembered her mom's lessons, she felt terribly inadequate to teach them to her brother. Pip would thrive in their new environment. He might even catch up on his language skills once he settled into a home and a routine that didn't involve watching his mom and sister get beaten up all the time.

It was happening. And Kimmie had done it. Her songs turned to psalms of praise.

Bless the Lord, o my soul, and all that's within me bless his holy name.

For the Lord is good, yes he is. The Lord is good, and his love endures forever.

I called on the Lord and he answered me. He saved me from my trouble.

Even though Kimmie had grown up singing these songs and listening to all of Mom's stories from the Bible, they'd never felt real to her until now. Kimmie was wrong to be angry at God for failing to answer her prayers. All this time, he'd been working out the details — all the way down to the electric company turning off their power and Chuck's having to use the outhouse — to secure their escape.

If only Mom had lived to see this day ...

But Kimmie couldn't think like that. Instead she shifted her thoughts to the future where she and Pip would have a nice place of their own. Nothing too outlandish. A two-bedroom townhouse would be fine. Anchorage had tons of parks. Her favorite playground while growing up sported a giant jungle gym, which was more colorful and complicated than what you could find at any of the other neighborhood parks. In fact, if she remembered right, that particular playground was located right across the street from a big apartment complex. That might be the perfect place to settle down, even more desirable than a townhouse. If she and Pip found a nice apartment, she wouldn't have to handle any of the snow shoveling or yard upkeep. It sounded better and better with each step that took them deeper into the woods.

Wait a minute. Wasn't she supposed to be leading Pip toward the Glenn? For as straight as the trail had seemed as she burrowed into the darkness to hide, she felt now like she'd been turned around a dozen different times like a kid spun around before hitting a piñata at a birthday party. This couldn't be right. She stared up at the sky. There was the big dipper, and if she were trained in navigation, she could probably use the North Star to figure out exactly where she was supposed to go from here, but the stellar map meant absolutely nothing to her now. It looked just like it had when she started her trek into the woods.

She stopped. "Hold on, Buster," she told her brother when he started to fidget. She checked to make sure his blanket was still wrapped tightly around his shoulders and then glanced up at the sky again. So that way was probably north ... But what did that tell her? She was so turned around she couldn't figure out which way she'd been walking, if she'd been walking in a single direction after all. While living at Chuck's trailer, the sun would rise above these woods, so did that mean she was supposed to head west to get back to the highway?

It was her best guess, but there were at least a dozen unknowns that kept her feet firmly planted where they were. What if the trail hadn't been as straight as she thought? What if turning around now meant landing straight back at Chuck's trailer? And since the Alaskan sun always rose at an angle and never due east, what did that mean for her calculations?

Not to mention the fact that she was only fifty percent sure that she'd figured out north correctly in the first place.

The temperature had dropped significantly when the last traces of sunlight disappeared, certainly not as bad as they'd get in the dead of winter, but this escape could have never happened in the dead of winter. It had to be now.

She held her brother close, borrowing a little of his warmth and refusing to accept that she might be lost. God wouldn't allow that to happen. He'd gotten her this far, which meant he wanted her to escape from Chuck's awful violence as much as she did. Which meant she would find her way to safety. The Lord would help her.

Wouldn't he?

She sank down with her back against a tree and held her

brother close. "Let's just rest for a minute here." She wanted to unwrap Pip and cozy up beside him under the blanket, but it was so cold out she didn't want him to lose all that warmth he'd stored up in his little portable burrow.

"You doing okay?" She didn't wait for an answer. She knew it wouldn't come.

"Ma."

She paused. "What?" Kimmie was cold, but she was certain she wasn't imagining things. She stared into her brother's face. "What did you say?" She held her breath, waiting.

Nothing.

"Were you talking about Mommy?" Kimmie prodded, refusing to admit the sound might have been a random vocalization.

Pip stared at her blankly. He was tired. He should have been in a warm bed sleeping, not tramping through the woods. She pulled his blanket more tightly around his shoulders. "Do you miss Mommy?" she asked. Up until she said those words, she'd thought she'd been doing fine, but mentioning their mother brought a massive lump to her dry throat. She needed water. Pip must too, but there wasn't anything they could do until they got out of these woods.

Which meant she couldn't sit here wondering if her brother,

whom everyone had considered nonverbal for the first three years of his life, had just spoken his first word or not.

She had to keep going. The more they moved, the more heat they would generate and the closer they'd get to the trooper's station.

The closer they'd get to safety.

Hopefully.

She stood up, glancing in all directions to make sure she was still on the same path she'd been on when she decided to stop. She couldn't be entirely sure that this would be the way to lead them to the trooper's station or not, but there was only one way to find out.

"Come on, Buster." She tried to make her voice sound as cheerful as possible. "Let's go see what's down this trail."

CHAPTER 25

If Kimmie had been able to plan her escape better, she would have left earlier in the month, before the termination dust fell, before the nights grew so frozen. Thankfully, it was clear out, and the moon kept the woods illuminated, but without the cloud covering, the night was bitter cold. She and her brother had no protection but a light windbreaker and one tattered blanket, and they were lost.

Kimmie was certain of it. She'd long lost track of the time, but it seemed to her that by now the moon was already on its way down in the sky. Which meant she'd been walking for several hours along the path she thought should have led her back to the Glenn Highway, and she had no idea where they were.

"Let's stop here for a minute, Buster."

Pip hadn't made any sounds for quite a while, no whining or whimpering. He'd stumbled a few times until Kimmie started to worry he was falling asleep while he walked. She tried carrying him but had to put him down every few minutes.

This wasn't going to work.

She was sweating beneath her jacket, even though her exposed face and hands burned with cold. She couldn't keep this up. It was too much for her. She was too tired.

She stopped to listen. If she could just hear one car or truck heading down the Glenn, she'd know which direction to turn. She'd been straining her ears for what felt like hours, but the Glenn was hardly traveled at this time of night, especially this far past tourist season. She heard the occasional rustling of wind, which only meant she had to brace herself for another onslaught of icy chill. Her legs ached, the pain in her feet reminding her that she and her brother had been walking way longer than they should have. How far was she into the woods now? She might be a hundred yards from the Glenn and wouldn't know it in this darkness, or she might be miles in the opposite direction.

What would happen if they didn't find their way out? She was too exhausted to carry Pip any farther. Each time she stopped to rest, she had to guess which way she'd most recently come from. Her mind was foggy, and even though it was convenient that Pip wasn't complaining or acting scared, she was worried by his complacency and her own mental confusion.

She held her brother close, and he nestled his cheek against hers. Her face was so cold she could hardly feel his skin. A moment later, his deep breathing told her he was asleep, and she wanted nothing more than to curl up beside him in their makeshift bed of spruce needles and forget herself until morning, but it was too cold. Neither of them would survive a night outside. Not if they stopped moving.

She watched her brother sleep, wondering how long she should wait before waking him up again. He needed his rest, but then again so did she. The problem was if she stayed here too long, she might lose the motivation to ever get herself back up. Then what would happen? Winter was closing in fast. What hikers would come out this way in that kind of weather? And the trappers who ventured this deep into the woods come wintertime might not even find their bodies if they were buried in snow or devoured by scavengers.

She tried to free herself from these oppressive fears, but they kept pressing in on her, weighing down on her chest, constricting her lungs until she felt like she could hardly breathe.

She had tried. God was her witness how hard she had tried. And in the end, it wasn't Chuck who did her in but this blasted cold and her own pathetic sense of direction. She thought of stories she'd heard of other unfortunate souls who met their demise in the Alaskan wilderness. Some were within a mile of the cabins or shelters or cell phone towers that might have saved them, but they had died nonetheless.

She couldn't let that happen to her and Pip. She had to find the energy to keep on going.

But not yet. After a short nap, she'd find her second wind. For now, she needed to rest. Just a few minutes, then she'd wake up.

Kimmie shut her eyes and let the heaviness and exhaustion sweep over her mind and carry her consciousness away into a merciful nothingness.

CHAPTER 26

She was at a birthday party in Anchorage. The kids were dressed up in pirate and princess costumes, laughing and drinking punch. Pip was sitting at the table, playing a puzzle game with two other little boys wearing eye patches and striped pants. He looked just as comfortable as the other children there, and even more amazing, he was laughing.

Kimmie excused herself from the chattering group of moms standing around with coffee cups in hand and stepped closer to her brother.

"My turn!" Pip exclaimed in a perfectly clear voice. "I get to go next."

Kimmie felt her entire core swelling with a pride so strong she wasn't sure her body could contain it all.

And then the fragments of her dream came crashing down around her like so many pieces of broken glass. She was awake. She was cold. And she was terrified.

"Pip!" she shook her brother, horrified by the feel of the

stiff blanket around him. "Pip!"

She had only meant to rest. How could she have been stupid enough to fall asleep? "Pip?"

She threw the blanket down from Pip's shoulder so she could search out his neck and try to find a pulse. Nausea swirled within her stomach, and her prayer came out in a terrified, pitiful plea. *Help us.*

He was alive. The relief she felt was enough to warm her body and shoot her mind into action. They couldn't stay here. And her brother couldn't sleep any longer.

"Come on, Pip. Let's go."

He was nearly impossible to rouse, but the way he scrunched up his face in complaint at Kimmie's vain attempts proved he was still alive. Still with her.

"Wake up, Buster," she begged. "We've got to keep walking."

She'd been so terrified by the fear that she'd let her brother die in the middle of the night that she hadn't looked around her at all. The aurora was out, not the glorious teals and purple lights that raced across the Glennallen skies in the dead of winter, but a dull green glow shining near the horizon.

It was the answer to all of her cumulative prayers. The northern lights almost always ran parallel to the Glenn, which meant that if she followed them straight on, she'd find her way to the highway.

"Let's go, Pip." This time she didn't have to fake her cheer or enthusiasm. Whispering a prayer of thanks, she planted her brother on his feet then when he started to whine picked him up, strengthened by her newfound hope.

She would get help soon. She and Pip were going to make it.

They would be safe.

They would be free.

CHAPTER 27

When Kimmie finally stumbled onto the Glenn Highway, she realized that she was miles from where she'd started her circuitous meandering through the woods. She'd never have the energy to get all the way to the trooper's station. Not now. Not like this. But it didn't matter. She was safe. She'd make it. She and Pip were going to be fine.

She'd been carrying her brother, and now as the northern lights faded back to darkness, her last remnants of strength melted away to a deep, nearly paralyzing exhaustion. She was so close. She just needed to get to a phone. Some place where she could call for help.

But where?

If it was the summer, she'd have the light of the midnight sun to guide her, with sleepy tourists on their way to Fairbanks or Canada making their way up the Glenn. But now there was nothing. If it were the weekend, she might run into hunters coming back home with their spoils, but the night was dark and the highway deserted.

"It's okay," she told herself, speaking softly as if she were giving her sleeping brother a pep talk. "We're going to make it."

Walking to the trooper's station would take her too close to her stepfather's neighborhood. It wasn't worth the risk of getting caught. If Chuck was out looking for her, she shouldn't even be this close to the highway in the first place. Besides, she couldn't make it that whole distance. Not as cold and weak as she was.

The medical center was in the opposite direction, only a mile, maybe slightly more. It was a feasible distance to walk and still kept her away from Chuck's place. Besides, Pip really should get checked out. But with what money? Kimmie still didn't have her paperwork back from the state insurance she'd applied for, but it didn't matter. The people at the Copper River Clinic weren't going to turn her away.

She set her brother down. "Come on, Buster. Just a tiny bit more walking."

He made a miserable whine that was pitiful enough to wrench her soul apart, but she was at her physical limit.

"I can't carry you anymore," she tried to explain. "I just can't. Let's go see the nice doctor and get you taken care of,

130

okay?"

She was terrified of what the folks at Copper River would find when they took off his shoes. What if he had frostbite? What if they needed to amputate?

No, she wouldn't think like that. She and her brother could both still walk. They were just cold. The clinic probably saw patients like that on a regular basis and had fast and effective protocols all set to go. The idea of a steaming shower and layer after layer of thick electric blankets fueled her legs as she slowly plodded forward.

Her brain was past the point of exhaustion, past the point where she felt she'd break if she didn't get warmed up and rested soon. But she had to keep going, and she had to keep Pip awake. He had to make this last little walk. It couldn't be more than a mile to the clinic. They were so close.

She heard a car behind her, saw the headlights illuminating the darkness. It was still too far back to have seen her, at least she hoped it was. She grabbed Pip by the shoulders. Did she dare flag it down? Who would refuse to help a three-year-old child in the cold like this? But what if it was Chuck? What if he was coming after them? She turned but was so blinded by the headlights she had no idea what kind of vehicle was speeding toward her.

Pip stood frozen beside her as well. "Let's go!" she panted. "Down to the ravine."

She and Pip stumbled down the small hill, where she crouched with her arms around her brother until the car sped past.

It wasn't Chuck.

Stupid. What had she done? If she'd just had the courage to flag that driver down, she and Pip could be at the medical center in a minute or less. *Stupid.*

She vowed that if another car came this way, she was going to stand out in the middle of the road, waving her arms until it stopped. Even if it were Chuck, it was better to live under his tyranny than watch her brother die from hypothermia.

But no other cars came. She was on her own. Pip started crying. She guessed from the way he bounced back and forth that his feet were hurting. Was that just from walking all night, or had frostbite crept in?

Did frostbite even hurt? Her own feet were numb. Maybe it was a good sign that Pip felt something.

She couldn't carry him anymore, not in her arms like she had all night, but she couldn't watch him suffer like this either. She crouched down. "You'll have to climb on my back," she told him. That meant he couldn't have the blanket wrapped so

132

tightly around his body, but they'd have to manage as best they could. They were so close to help; it was going to be okay. They were both going to make it. They were so close now.

CHAPTER 28

Kimmie pressed the nighttime buzzer outside the Copper River Clinic's emergency room and nearly collapsed while she waited for the door to open. When a young nurse in Bugs Bunny scrubs opened the door, all Kimmie could manage to say was, "We got lost."

Soon she was sitting in a wheelchair, heavy blankets draped over her shoulders, her feet soaking in a warm bath. Pip sat in her lap while the physician's assistant checked his vitals.

"I think you're both very lucky to have made it out of those woods when you did." He looked at her meaningfully. "Is there anyone you need to call? Anyone who'll be worried about your safety?"

Kimmie's memory flashed to Taylor's card, still secure in her pocket, and she shook her head. "No. I just wanted to make sure he was ..." Her voice caught when she thought about what might have happened to Pip. "I just wanted him to come in to make sure he was all right."

134

The PA smiled. "Well, in that case I can relieve your worries. He's clearly hypothermic, but I don't see anything that's going to prevent either of you from a full recovery. If you'd stayed out much longer ..." He left the thought unfinished, and Kimmie was grateful. Pip had perked up once he was inside, and she didn't want him to hear anything that would cause undo alarm.

The PA wanted her and Pip to stay here a few more hours. Every so often, the nurse brought in hotter water to fill her foot bath. Pip was wrapped in layers of blankets, with hot water compresses tucked around his body while he sat on Kimmie's lap, and the nurse popped in every so often to get a new temperature reading. The PA told her that if she wanted, she and Pip could rest here until morning. She was badly in need of sleep, but she couldn't relax yet. Not until she saw with her own eyes that Pip's temperature was back to where it should be.

Everything had worked itself out in the end. Everything was going to be all right.

The PA stepped out for a minute, and Kimmie tried to figure out a way to get comfortable in her wheelchair. She didn't need it anymore, but it was the easiest way to keep Pip comfortable while she soaked her feet. She could think of worse things to worry about than starting tomorrow with a sore and stiff back.

She had just shut her eyes when someone knocked from outside her room. "Come in." Her voice was so weak, she doubted even Pip heard it let alone someone in the hallway. Her door swung open, and the nurse poked her head in, frowning apologetically.

"Someone's here to see you."

Kimmie's lungs seized up, and her heart rate soared. Chuck? How could he have found her? He had no idea where she and Pip were. What could she tell the nurse? How could she let them know not to let him in?

"It's a trooper," the woman announced, and Kimmie stared at her blankly.

A trooper?

The door opened wider, and Taylor stepped inside. He looked far more casual out of uniform but just as confident in his dark blue jeans and crisp flannel hanging open to reveal the vee-neck T-shirt beneath. He offered a smile that looked both tired and caring. "Sounds like you've had quite the adventure tonight."

Kimmie felt herself return his smile. "That's one way of putting it."

"You have a few minutes?" He ran his hand across the faint stubble on his jaw.

"Of course." She glanced around, trying to figure out where he could sit. Even without his trooper hat, Taylor was over six feet tall, and she felt like she'd get a kink in her neck if she had to stare up at him from this wheelchair for very long.

He reached out his long arm to shut the door then leaned against the exam table. He still wasn't sitting, but at least his relaxed posture made it easier for Kimmie to meet his eyes. He grinned at Pip. "How's the little guy? Is he doing okay?"

She nodded. "The PA says he'll be fine."

Taylor leveled his eyes. "And what about you?"

His question caught her off guard. Warmth flushed to her cheeks, warmth she probably couldn't attribute to her piles of blankets. "I'm fine, too. Thanks."

"Good. That's a real answer to prayer."

She waited for him to say more, still slightly confused why he was here. How had he heard about what happened to Pip and her unless Chuck had called the station when he found them missing? And what did it mean that he wasn't in uniform? Was he working tonight, or had he heard she was here and come in to check on her?

He reached down and brushed some hair off of Pip's forehead. "You look tired, little buddy."

Pip blinked his drooping eyelids once before they closed

shut. Kimmie was relieved to feel him relax in her arms.

"I just got out of a meeting with your sister." Taylor's words didn't make any sense. Her sister?

"She's here? In Glennallen?"

Taylor nodded. "She showed up at your home to check on you. Your stepdad told her you were already asleep and refused to let her in, but she had a bad feeling about it all. She went around to the window and saw your empty room from the outside. She said there was also a rifle poking out from under the mattress."

Kimmie tried not to blush. She thought she'd done a better job hiding it.

Taylor was staring at her with a gaze full of compassion. "Are you still cold?"

She hadn't realized until then she'd started shivering. The nurse said it might happen as her body regained heat, but she suspected the reaction had more to do with the thought of her sister sneaking around Chuck's trailer like some sort of amateur sleuth. Meg had no idea what kind of man she was dealing with. What was she thinking? If Chuck had found her snooping through the windows, who knew what he might have done?

"I'm all right." Kimmie smiled in an attempt to appear more convincing. "It's just been a really long, hard night." She

138

swallowed down the lump that had formed in her throat. Why did it always feel like when she was with Taylor she was going to break down into tears? He was strong and confident, the kind of man who should make a woman feel at ease. Instead, his strength only heightened her own sense of vulnerability, and the compassion and gentleness of his demeanor reminded her that she and Pip deserved so much more love and happiness than life had given them.

Taylor leaned forward and tucked in one of the blankets that had fallen off Pip's shoulder. "Here." He wrapped Kimmie and her sleeping brother closer together. "Is that better?" As he pulled away, the back of his hand brushed against her cheek. She jumped involuntarily.

If he noticed her reaction, he didn't show it.

Taylor sat in the PA's swivel chair. Rolling it a little closer to her, he held her gaze steady. "A lot of people were really worried for your safety."

She tried to read from his expression if he'd been one of them.

He lowered his voice. "Can you tell me what happened tonight?" She didn't know what he was asking. She had no idea how to respond. What did Taylor already know? What did he suspect? According to the story Kimmie told the clinic staff, she and Pip had gone for a walk to look at the stars and gotten lost in the woods. It was on the far side of believable, but nobody had asked for any corroborating details.

Taylor looked stern. "I want to help you, Kimmie. And I think you need it."

She didn't bother contradicting him. It was true. She had risked her life tonight to get Pip to safety. Now here she was, only a few miles from home, but she was with someone who could help her. Taylor would know what to do.

"You don't have to be afraid." He reached out and took her hand. It wasn't until she felt the steadiness of his touch that she realized how much she was trembling. "You can trust me." His voice was earnest. "I want to help you."

She glanced down at her brother, soundly asleep in her arms, reminding herself that she would do anything to keep him safe.

Kimmie told Taylor everything.

CHAPTER 29

Kimmie was shaking so hard that a few minutes into her story Taylor reached over and helped her settle Pip onto the hospital bed. "I don't want you to drop him," he explained gently.

Kimmie felt even more vulnerable and exposed without her brother on her lap. It was as if her entire body was a window into the pit of her psyche, and as long as she had Pip shielding her, the curtains were at least partially drawn. Now there was nothing to separate her and Taylor, nothing to filter out the awful truth.

She clutched her blankets around her shoulders and told him everything, not just about tonight when Chuck had threatened her with a rifle but all that she and her mom had endured. Horror stories she hadn't recalled in years came tumbling out like a tangled mass of words, but instead of bringing healing and catharsis, she felt defiled having to relive those haunting memories, victimized all over again in the retelling.

Taylor was a patient listener, asking a few pointed questions that kept Kimmie focused, making compassionate *mmm*s at the right times, nodding his head in sympathy. When Kimmie had drained her memory banks completely dry, Taylor held her gaze. "Thank you for being honest with me. I'm sure that wasn't easy."

She was still trembling, but he didn't mention it. She stared at him, wondering what was supposed to happen now. She'd done her job. She'd gotten Pip out of Chuck's house and managed to tell the trooper about all the abuse they'd suffered. Her mission, as gruesome and excruciating as it was, had been a success.

Taylor sighed heavily in his chair, and Kimmie wondered if she'd depressed him with her stories. He was so engaged while she was talking, but now that everything was disclosed, he looked tired. For a second, she wondered if she'd made a mistake. What if he came back and said there was nothing he could do? If not even a state trooper could free her brother from Chuck, her dreams of freedom and safety were nothing but an illusion.

The thought led to a terrifying conclusion.

What if Taylor couldn't help her? What if he told her it was out of his jurisdiction? What if he told her that since Pip himself hadn't been the victim of physical abuse, he had to go back home and live with his dad?

Kimmie braced herself, certain that the next words out of Taylor's mouth would tell her that everything she'd suffered through tonight was in vain. She and her brother would never be free.

Instead, he reached out toward Pip, who'd rolled out of his blankets, and tucked him back in carefully. Taylor looked at Kimmie with a gaze full of sympathy and trust. "I'm glad you were able to talk about these things. All your stories are going to help us build our case."

"What case?"

Taylor was gazing at Pip while he slept peacefully in the hospital bed. "The case against your stepfather. We've put out the warrant for his arrest."

"Because you thought he hurt us and that's why we were missing when my sister came by?"

Taylor shook his head. "No. Because we've received solid evidence that implicates him in your mother's murder."

CHAPTER 30

Kimmie stared at the trooper, wondering why Taylor's words didn't cause any of the emotional reactions she might have expected.

"So you found proof?" She realized that she sounded clinical and unmoved, but that's also how she felt. Taylor suspected that Chuck was involved in her mom's death. Was she truly surprised, or was he simply telling her the truth that she'd been trying to deny?

He nodded. "Your sister ... well, maybe I should let her explain it to you."

Kimmie wished he wouldn't. Taylor would never understand the kind of relationship she had with Meg. "I think I'd rather hear it from you," she admitted, hoping she didn't sound too rude.

He nodded in understanding. "Well, I guess your mom was making plans with your sister. Meg was going to drive out to Glennallen to pick up you and your mom and your brother and take you to her house in Anchorage." He leveled his gaze. "Your mom was getting ready to leave Chuck."

No matter how much Kimmie might have wanted to believe those words in the past, she still couldn't believe them to be true. Mom was scared. She was timid. How would Meg have convinced her to find the courage to leave?

Jumbled thoughts and half-formed arguments raced chaotically through Kimmie's mind. Meg had always disliked their stepfather. She could have made something up. If Mom were ever going to leave Chuck, it would have happened years earlier, before things got as bad as they had. Meg didn't know what she was talking about. She was just trying to find a way to take charge over the family that she'd abandoned so long ago.

Of course, Kimmie would be stupid to defend Chuck of all people. He'd certainly shown himself over the years capable of a rage that could turn murderous, but there was a part of her brain that still wanted to believe Mom decided to end her life on her own terms. If Chuck really had killed Mom, there must have been something Kimmie could have done to intervene. Something she could have changed. She could have fought harder to get Mom out of that trailer. She could have told somebody about the abuse that was going on back when she was in high school. Her teachers would have had to get protective services involved. Kimmie could have done something differently.

She could have saved her mother.

"Are you all right?" Taylor asked. "It's a lot to take in."

She wanted to yell at him. Wanted to scream that her sister was a liar. But Meg had no reason to make a story like this up. Hadn't she told Kimmie she had more information about Mom's death?

Taylor wrapped his arm around her, which only made her tremble harder. "I'm so sorry," he whispered. "But the good news is you're here now. You and your brother are both going to be safe."

"So you found him then?" Kimmie asked.

Taylor shook his head. "He wasn't home when our men went by earlier, but don't worry. Soon your stepfather will be behind bars, right where he belongs."

Kimmie looked into Taylor's kind and earnest eyes and trusted him.

She didn't have any other choice.

CHAPTER 31

"Thank God you're safe." Meg threw her arms around Kimmie's shoulders in the hotel lobby then flung a smile at Taylor. "Thank you so much, officer, for all you've done for our family. You're an angel."

Kimmie bristled at the flirtatious tone her married sister had adopted, and she reached for her brother, asleep in Taylor's arms. "I can take him from here."

Taylor shook his head. "You've had enough physical exertion for the day, I think. Let me carry him up to your room. It's no problem."

Meg draped her hands over his bicep and crooned, "You're right. I bet to you he's no heavier than a piece of paper, right?"

Taylor smiled and raised his eyebrows at Kimmie as if to ask, *is your sister always like this?*

She shrugged. *Unfortunately, yes.*

Meg led the way up the hotel staircase and to their room on the second floor, past several moose and caribou heads mounted on the wall, their sad and mournful eyes seeming to follow the procession. Meg fumbled with her key card, laughing airily when she realized she'd been trying to insert it upside-down.

"Which bed is his?" Taylor asked. Kimmie glanced at the two doubles in their room. If Chuck found out where they were hiding and barged into the hotel, where would Pip be safest? A dozen scenarios ran through her head, pictures of her stepfather breaking into their room, rifle aimed to kill.

"Let's settle him down here." Kimmie pulled down the blankets on the bed by the window, but Meg shook her head.

"You don't want him sleeping that close to the heater, do you? It can't be good for his breathing, all that dust blowing around in the air. Why don't you put him here? He'll stay warmer if he doesn't catch a draft."

Taylor looked from one sister to the other, still holding Pip in his arms. He raised his eyebrows questioningly at Kimmie.

"Fine," she answered. "He can sleep there."

Meg grinned smugly as Taylor lowered Pip into the bed by the door. Kimmie would sleep on the other side of him, so at least if Chuck barged in he'd have to get through her first.

Was this what her life was reduced to? Hiding from Chuck in a cheap hotel room, wondering when he'd attack? Maybe she'd feel better when they got to Anchorage. But would she

148

ever be truly safe?

Meg stepped between her and Taylor. "Thanks again for all you've done, officer. You're so brave. I'm just so thankful we have people like you looking out for all us little guys." She let out another girlish giggle.

Kimmie studied Taylor's expression, trying to figure out if he was the kind of guy who would immediately fall under Meg's dazzling spell. Twenty-seven and rich enough to afford her own personal trainer and year-long visits to the tanning booth, Meg looked like she came off the pages of a beauty magazine even wearing her simple designer jeans and casual blouse that clung tightly to her figure.

Surprisingly, Taylor offered a quick word of thanks then turned his attention to Kimmie. "Are you going to be all right here for the night?"

She thought it was weird that he was asking her. Wasn't it his job to know how safe she was? Shouldn't he be able to answer that question far more readily than she would?

"We'll leave for Anchorage first thing tomorrow." Meg took a step closer to him and flung her shoulders back. Kimmie wondered if her sister realized how silly she looked trying to catch the gaze of a near stranger or if her filthy-rich husband had any idea how she acted around other men when he wasn't around.

Taylor glanced at Pip curled up on the hotel bed, and Kimmie watched his gentle features soften even more. "I think that's good." He was talking to Kimmie, staring at her now with an intensity that made her face heat up. "You'll be safe in Anchorage. Does Chuck know where your sister lives?"

"I don't know how he could," Meg answered, clearly waiting for this chance to insert herself into the conversation. "He never let Mom come and visit. I don't think Mom even had my address."

"That's good." Taylor looked relieved. He lowered his voice, leaning in toward Kimmie. "Do you still have my cell number?"

She nodded. Kimmie didn't have to put her hand in her pocket to know it was there. All night long, she'd been fingering its wrinkled corners, trying to muster up the last of her courage and strength while she was trying to lead Pip out of those cold woods.

Taylor smiled. "Why don't you give me a call once you feel settled and let me know how you're doing."

Behind him, Meg raised her sculpted eyebrows, and her mouth dropped open into a tiny O before spreading into a grin that made Kimmie feel queasy.

"Officer," Meg sang out in her most melodic voice, "I'm sure it's going to be hard for Kimmie to leave everything she knows behind here in Glennallen. I bet it'd be a real treat for her if you'd come have dinner with us one night. We're up on the hillside, and we'd love to have you."

Kimmie wanted to join her brother in bed and throw the blankets over her face, but Taylor was still gazing straight at her, holding her captive by the intensity of his stare. "I'd like that," he said.

Kimmie ignored the sloshing feeling in her gut, the skipping and erratic heartbeat in her chest. He'd fallen prey to Meg's charm, and that was all. There wasn't a single member of the male species who could refuse her anything.

Meg was wiggling her eyebrows up and down when Taylor wasn't looking. Kimmie had no idea what information her sister was trying to convey or why she was making such a fool of herself. Whatever it was she suspected, Meg was reading the situation wrong. Taylor wouldn't drive all the way to Anchorage just to visit some fancy home on the hillside. He was only saying that to be nice, the same way an adult smiles at the little kid who says they're going to grow up to become an astronaut or the president. Taylor was doing what any polite person in his situation would do, but unless he had to relay more information regarding her stepfather's case, Kimmie knew she wouldn't see him again.

Meg had no idea how much she was humiliating herself when she put her manicured fingers on Taylor's shoulder and giggled, "It's a date then."

Kimmie wanted to apologize for her sister's behavior, but when she found the courage to glance at Taylor's face, she was surprised to find a gentle bemusement where she expected to see impatience or irritation.

"Funny coincidence," he said. "But tomorrow's my day off, and in the afternoon, I've got to drive my friend to the airport. Any chance you ladies would be free around six?"

"Tomorrow?" Meg asked.

Taylor looked at the alarm clock by Pip's bedside. "Actually, it's today if you wanted to be technical."

Kimmie had about two dozen different arguments. She and Pip were still exhausted. A few hours of sleep in a strange hotel followed by a four-hour drive to her sister's wasn't going to leave anybody with energy to play hostess. Pip would be confused enough being in a new place surrounded by new people. The last thing he needed was Taylor stealing Kimmie's attention away from where it really needed to be.

Kimmie shot her sister an imploring look, one she was

certain Meg was going to ignore.

Meg frowned. "I'm sorry, officer. My husband's in real estate. He's got a really important meeting at six tomorrow that we can't miss."

Relief washed over Kimmie's whole body until her sister's face broke out into a mischievous grin. "But while Dwayne and I are out, I'm sure Kimmie's free. Why don't the two of you have dinner together?"

Each and every argument that ran through her brain died on Kimmie's lips when Taylor leaned slightly toward her. "I'd like that. I'll bring takeout. Does Pip like Chinese food?"

Did he? If it wasn't chili from a can, white bread, or one of the frozen meals he ate at the daycare, Pip had likely never tried it.

"You've got my number." Taylor continued to smile. He looked so genuinely happy Kimmie couldn't bring herself to mutter some excuse to free him from this embarrassing arrangement. "Why don't you plan on texting me your sister's address once you and Pip are settled."

She refused to tell him she didn't even have a cell phone and had never sent a text in her life. For all the joy her sister derived from playing matchmaker, Meg could lend Kimmie her phone for something as simple as that.

Meg flung her hair over her shoulder like she was auditioning for a shampoo commercial. "Well, then, it's a date. We'll see you tomorrow night."

Kimmie plopped onto the bed as soon as Taylor closed the hotel room door behind him. Meg sank down next to her and elbowed her in the ribs. "Well, come on now, a date with Officer Chiseled? No need to thank me. Just be sure to invite me to the wedding."

Kimmie pulled the blankets over her head. She was dying to sleep, but if truth were to be told, she was too embarrassed to let Meg see the girly grin that had spread across her face.

CHAPTER 32

That night, Kimmie dreamed she was strapped in the passenger seat of a car speeding recklessly over a bridge. "Slow down," she shouted at the driver.

Chuck's menacing laugh answered back. "You think this is fast, girlie? You haven't seen fast yet."

Pip squealed in the back seat, but Kimmie's seatbelt was so tight it was digging into her shoulder bone. She couldn't turn around to offer her brother any comfort.

"You're scaring him," she yelled, hoping Chuck would feel some degree of pity for his own child. Instead, he laughed again, filling the front seat of the car with the scent of stale beer and sunflower seeds.

"How's this for scared?" He spun the wheel back and forth, sending their speeding car careening from one lane to the other. The bridge swayed beneath them. Kimmie gripped her seat, praying for rescue. If she reached out, if she were able to seize hold of the wheel ... No, it was too dangerous. There was nothing to do. Nothing to do but pray and wait and hope that she and Pip survived.

She woke up drenched in sweat. Meg was staring down at her with a frown. "Sorry to wake you, sleeping beauty, but if I'm going to get my house ready for your hot date tonight, we need to get on the road."

Kimmie glanced at the clock. Seven thirty? After everything they'd gone through last night, Meg thought it was appropriate to wake her and Pip up at seven thirty?

"Come on," Meg urged. "I've got a hair appointment in town at noon, and I don't want to cancel."

Kimmie rolled her eyes. At least Meg's real reason for waking her up this early was more in line with her character, easier for Kimmie to accept. She glanced at her sleeping brother, hating to break his rest.

Meg flung a suitcase on the bed and started to fill it. "Let's go. He can sleep in the car."

Kimmie didn't have the energy to argue. Besides, she and Pip probably shouldn't linger in Glennallen any longer than was necessary, not with Chuck still running loose. She reached out her arm to give her brother a gentle shake. "Come on, Buster. Time to wake up."

"You call him Buster?" Meg paused with a pair of heels in

her hands. Who packs heels to take a four-hour drive to do nothing but pick up their sister?

Kimmie continued to focus on Pip. "Yeah. Why?"

"That's what Mom used to call Dad when they were being silly. Don't you remember?"

Kimmie shook her head. Back when they'd lived together, one of Meg's favorite pastimes was playing *Don't you remember*, a game in which Meg received the inherent bragging rights that came from having far more recollections about their dad than Kimmie ever would. The superiority that went along with her status as *eldest daughter with the best memory* was as infuriating as it was unjust. Why should Meg be the one with all the memories?

"Hey, is he always this hard to wake up?" Meg asked, studying Kimmie and her failed attempts to rouse Pip.

She shrugged. "Not always. But he's had a hard night." There was an edge in her voice she didn't try to mask. What did her sister expect? Meg had no idea what Pip had gone through lately, and she never would. Yet another case of Meg's getting all the family's allotted dose of good luck. It wasn't enough for her to be the prettiest, the smartest, and the one with all the memories of Dad. She was also the one who'd never had to deal with Chuck, never had to clean up his snotty paper towels or fetch his coffee sludge. As far as Kimmie knew, Meg had never been hit a day in her life, and her most pressing worry was whether or not she could keep her figure trim enough to warrant her position as a trophy bride for one of Anchorage's most successful real estate moguls.

"Maybe you should just take the blankets off him and let the cold wake him up."

Kimmie glared at her sister. Did driving four hours to meet her half-brother make Meg some kind of parenting expert all of a sudden?

"Come on, Pip," Kimmie pleaded. "You've got to wake up."

"If you keep snuggling him like that, he won't have any reason to get out of bed."

Kimmie ignored Meg's nagging, and eventually her sister took the hint and went back to her packing. Kimmie brushed Pip's forehead. "Does he feel hot to you?"

Meg reached out then shrugged. "Little bit, but you've kept him buried under those blankets all night."

"I wonder if he's getting sick. It wouldn't be a surprise after he spent so much time outside."

Meg rolled her eyes. "Is that still what they're teaching in these Glennallen schools? The cold can't make you sick. It doesn't work that way. It's just an old wives' tale."

"Shut up." Kimmie flung the blankets off her brother. The PA at the clinic hadn't warned Kimmie about overheating. Had she bundled him too tightly in her worry for his safety?

"I'm serious," Meg went on. "If anything, all the cold does is lower your immunity. It can't actually give you a virus."

"I said shut up." Kimmie stood Pip on the ground and watched anxiously while he blinked his sleepy eyes awake. "Are you all right, Buster?" She wished Meg hadn't mentioned that being one of their mom's pet names for their dad. She was going to feel self-conscious now each and every time she used it. "Pip? Are you all right?"

He scrunched up his face.

"I think he needs to see a doctor," Kimmie announced.

Meg threw a fancy handbag into her suitcase. "He's probably just tired."

"He looks like he's in pain."

Meg shrugged. "That's how I look every morning before I put on my makeup."

I bet it is, Kimmie thought to herself. She sat down on the edge of their bed and took Pip into her arms. "Does something hurt," she asked him, "or are you just tired, buddy?"

He winced.

"Can you show me what hurts?" Kimmie ignored her

159

sister's melodramatic sigh. Meg was probably worried about that hair appointment she'd miss if they didn't get on the road soon. Hair like that probably had to be touched up once or twice a month. With as much as Meg was sure to be paying her stylist, the hairdresser could afford to reschedule.

"Something's really wrong. I think we better get him checked out."

"Fine," Meg huffed as she zipped her overstuffed suitcase shut. "But you don't want to take him to this Glennallen hole in wall. I mean, it's fine for something like last night when you need quick attention right away, but for childhood illnesses, you really should see a specialist. Does that tiny little clinic here even have a pediatrician on staff?"

Kimmie had spent all of Pip's life worrying herself sick over every minor injury or sniffle, hating that his father was too cheap to allow him to get proper medical care. Now that Chuck was out of the picture, there was no way Kimmie was going to relinquish her decision-making authority, handing the responsibility over to someone who hardly even knew her brother.

"The Copper River Clinic's closest," she argued. "Let's just stop by there on the way out of town." She thought about the Cole twins who'd been out of the daycare with strep throat and hoped Pip hadn't picked up something like that.

She put her finger on his chin. "Open your mouth like this. "Let me take a look."

"Good grief, Kimberly," Meg whined. "You're not a nurse."

No, but I'm his sister, which is more than you're acting like at the moment. She kept the retort unspoken and tried to look in Pip's mouth.

All she could see was black. "You have a flashlight or something?"

Meg crossed her arms. "Do you even know what you're looking for? Does working part-time at a daycare all of a sudden make you an expert in childhood illnesses?"

"Do you have a flashlight or not?" she repeated. "All I need is a simple yes or no."

Meg rolled her eyes. "Use my cell." She tossed her phone onto the blanket and then let out a loud and frustrated sigh when Kimmie asked her how to turn on the light.

"I can't believe you don't even know how to use a cell phone."

Kimmie ignored the remark. "Now say 'ah,'" she told her brother.

"Do you even know if he understands a word you're saying?" Meg asked as she stared into the mirror above the dresser applying her mascara.

Kimmie heard the question, but as she shined the light, she realized Meg was right about one thing. She really didn't know what she was looking for. Pip's throat was bright red, but maybe that's the color it always was.

She tried to figure out how to turn the light off when Meg finally yanked it out of her hands and did it herself. "Did you find what you were looking for?"

Kimmie ignored her sister's sarcasm. "I want to take him to the clinic before we head out of town."

"If you wait a few hours, I have a friend with a kid about that age. I actually borrowed her car seat for Pip's drive to Anchorage. She takes her son to a naturopath in Eagle River, says she's a miracle worker."

"I don't want a naturopath," Kimmie snapped. "And I don't need a miracle worker. I just want someone to check him out and let me know if something's wrong."

"Of course something's wrong," Meg replied. "The kid's three and doesn't even talk yet. Which reminds me, I have a number for you to call once we get you settled in. There's a state program for kids with special needs, where they'll come right to your house."

"That's not what I'm talking about." Kimmie wondered how

she and her sister would survive the long drive to Anchorage, let alone coexist under the same roof until Kimmie found a place of her own. It was a good thing Meg had a mansion where they'd have plenty of space so hopefully Kimmie and her brother could keep to themselves.

Meg stared at Kimmie, who felt like she was now expected to apologize for her outburst. Instead she gave Pip a little squeeze, straightened out his rumpled clothes, and said, "Let's find where that nice trooper put your shoes last night and then we'll take a quick visit to say hi to the nurse." She shot a look at her sister, who managed to roll her eyes while applying her eye makeup.

"Fine with me. While you're in with the nurse PA or whoever they've got working there, I guess I'll call my hairstylist and cancel that appointment."

CHAPTER 33

The clinic was only a few minutes away from the hotel, but Kimmie was shaking by the time Meg pulled up in front of the building. She didn't know if it was her body reliving last night's trauma or the adrenaline in her system from fighting with her sister. Maybe both.

"You coming in?" she asked Meg, who was still buckled in the driver's seat.

"Go on ahead. I've got some phone calls to make." Meg adjusted the rearview mirror so she could look at herself as she reapplied her lipstick. Ignoring her, Kimmie helped Pip out of his car seat. "Come on, Buster," she whispered in his ear. "Let's see if the nurses here can do anything to help you feel better."

After checking her brother in, Kimmie sat down with Pip on her lap and started reading a magazine. In the corner, two kids around Pip's age were playing in the children's area, stacking blocks and coloring while their mom scrolled on her cell phone.

Kimmie was exhausted. One nice thing about driving all the

164

way to Anchorage with Meg was her sister was a coffee snob and probably knew the best place in the area to get a hot drink.

"Well, fancy seeing you two here."

Kimmie turned around at the familiar voice as a smile worked its way to her lips. "Look, Pip. It's Trooper Tanner."

"Call me Taylor, okay?" He stood above them, staring down in a way that reminded Kimmie just how tall he was. He grinned and sat down next to her, and she wondered if she smelled as gross and looked as tired as she suspected.

Taylor reached over and offered a playful pout to Pip, who was frowning and leaning against Kimmie's chest. "Everything all right?"

"He woke up with a little bit of a fever," she explained.

Taylor tousled Pip's hair. "Poor little thing."

Kimmie wondered what else she was supposed to say. It wasn't like she had any practice running into handsome troopers in doctor's offices, but she figured it wasn't polite to ask something like, "So, what are you doing here?" She stared at her hands resting on Pip's legs.

"Did you both sleep okay at the hotel?" Taylor asked.

She nodded, pressing her lips together, trying to figure out why her brain had suddenly grown incapable of carrying on a simple conversation. Behind them, the two kids argued over a broken crayon until their mom barked at them.

Taylor stretched out his legs, looking perfectly at ease. "So, we still on for dinner tonight?"

Kimmie flushed. "Oh, I'm sorry about that. My sister can be kind of a handful."

"Well, that doesn't seem like something you need to apologize for, does it?" Taylor asked with a grin.

"No." She tried to smile. "I just didn't want you to feel like you were forced into anything you didn't want to do."

Taylor chuckled. "I hate driving to Anchorage. I rarely go in. I'm only doing it because I owe my buddy a pretty big favor. He doesn't have anyone else to take him in time to catch his flight."

"Does he need a ride?" Kimmie asked. "We've got room in the back seat."

Taylor shook his head. "That's not what I meant. I wasn't asking you to drive him in. I'm just saying that knowing I'll be ending the day with you and your brother and some great Chinese food is going to keep me from getting grumpy on the road."

Kimmie smiled and forced herself to look away before her flush deepened.

"Pippin Jenkins?" The nurse called out. "Ready for you

now."

Kimmie set her brother down and stood up, facing Taylor. "Well, I guess I'll see you tonight." She felt silly stretching out her hand as if she were an applicant who'd just finished a job interview, but Taylor pressed it warmly.

"I'll be looking forward to this evening." His smile made her warmer than she'd been all fall.

As she walked with Pip toward the nurse, she felt Taylor's kind gaze following them, somewhat surprised to realize that she was looking forward to their dinner tonight just as much as he was.

CHAPTER 34

"We'll get those results from the strep test back in a few minutes," the PA explained. Kimmie was still sweating from having to hold Pip down while the physician's assistant tried to swab the back of his throat.

Tabitha scowled at her pad of paper. "May as well write him a prescription now, because I can pretty much guarantee it's going to come back positive."

Kimmie felt much more comfortable with the PA she met last night than the one examining Pip today. Tabitha was old and ill-humored and made Kimmie wonder if she had outlived her lifetime dose of both compassion and bedside manners. She stopped scribbling and looked up.

"How old did you say your son is?"

Kimmie had explained earlier that Pip was her brother, but this was the second time since then Tabitha had made the same mistake. It wasn't worth correcting the PA again, so Kimmie just answered, "Three."

Tabitha still stood, frozen, with her pen poised over her pad. "Three years and how many months?"

"He'll turn four in November."

Tabitha narrowed her eyes. "Three years, ten months." She glared at him while emphasizing these last two words.

"Ten months?" Kimmie repeated. "Yeah, I guess that's right."

The way Tabitha rolled her eyes reminded Kimmie of how her sister might look in another forty years if she ran out of money for all her anti-aging skin treatments.

"And he doesn't talk at all?" Tabitha asked.

Kimmie searched for a polite way to remind the provider that her patient was sitting right in front of her, listening in.

"He does use some words," Kimmie stated defensively, stretching the truth just a little.

Tabitha raised a single eyebrow. "Single words, I assume?"

Kimmie stared at her blankly.

"He's not stringing words together yet to form sentences?" the PA pressed.

Kimmie shook her head, feeling just as ashamed as her brother would be if he understood this conversation. "No sentences. Not yet," she added as a hopeful aside.

Tabitha reached for a brochure. "And who's his

pediatrician? You're taking him to someone in town, I assume?"

Kimmie felt far too intimidated and bewildered to admit that Pip had never seen a healthcare provider until his trip to the emergency room last night. "There's a naturopath in Eagle River," she answered, careful to word her statement in a way that was not technically a lie.

"Well," Tabitha went on, "I'm sure I have no idea if a naturopath utilizes the same developmental screening methods as a real doctor, but it's clear to me that this child is lacking in his development and could benefit from speech intervention services."

She reached into a drawer and pulled out a brochure. "In all honesty, I was surprised when you told me he wasn't receiving any therapy already. They'll do free home visits through the state for all income brackets," she added, carefully eyeing Kimmie.

She took the brochure with a humble, "Thanks," and was relieved when a nurse popped in.

"The test came back positive," he announced.

Tabitha nodded at him with a smug look then handed Kimmie a prescription form covered in scribbles. "Take this to the pharmacy. Expect it to take them ten or fifteen minutes to get everything ready. Follow the directions on the bottle, and you really should make that call for speech services. Most experts say that intervention before the age of two is most ideal. After that the window of opportunity shrinks exponentially as a child ages."

Shutting her ears to Tabitha's ominous prognosis, Kimmie sighed with relief when the PA stepped out.

Kimmie ran her hand across Pip's forehead. "You doing all right, Buster?" She searched his face for clues that might indicate how much, if any, of the conversation with Tabitha he'd understood. Kimmie knew there was far more to her brother than the PA gave him credit for, but she also knew that Tabitha was probably right about some things. If Kimmie had known Pip could get free speech therapy through the state, she would have convinced her mom to make it happen. Instead of a home visit, maybe the specialist could have worked with Pip at the daycare. How much farther along might he be if Chuck hadn't kept them slaves in his trailer, unable to reach out to anybody on the outside for help?

She shouldn't have wasted precious minutes in the waiting room, staring at Taylor, acting like a starstruck schoolgirl. She should have been telling the trooper more about Chuck, helping with the investigation by brainstorming where in the world her stepdad might be hiding out. At least she'd be seeing Taylor again tonight. This time, instead of acting like a stupefied idiot, Kimmie would do everything she could to help him with the case. She would make sure that Chuck was never free to hurt her or her brother again.

CHAPTER 35

Leading Pip back toward the lobby, Kimmie heard her sister's abrasive giggle even before she stepped into the waiting room. What was Meg doing? Didn't she know how rude it was to talk that loudly on the phone in a public area?

Except that Meg wasn't on the phone.

Her sister stood and smiled brilliantly when Kimmie stepped forward. "So," Meg said, drumming her perfectly shaped, long fingernails on Taylor's shoulder, "you're back. Did the doctor give you the answers you wanted?"

Kimmie fought back an unjustified wave of jealousy when she saw her sister with Taylor. "Pip's got strep." She shot a haughty glance at Meg.

"Poor little guy." Taylor reached out and ran his fingers gently through Pip's hair.

"Well, you ready to go?" Meg adjusted the strap of her handbag and glanced at the clock hanging above the pharmacy window.

"No," Kimmie answered, "I've got to wait for Pip's medicine."

Meg sat back down next to Taylor and bumped her shoulder against his. "I guess it's a busy day at the pharmacy then, isn't it?"

"I'm waiting to get a prescription filled too," he explained. He patted the empty chair next to him. "Have a seat."

Kimmie held up the piece of paper Tabitha had given her. "I think I need to drop this off first." She would never admit it in front of her sister, but she was glad someone was here who knew how to use a pharmacy. She found herself wondering what kind of medicine someone as strong and apparently healthy as Taylor needed and fought down another surge of jealousy as she realized that her sister was so nosy that it was probably the very first question she'd asked him.

Taylor showed her where to drop off Pip's prescription, and then she sat down next to him, waiting. Hadn't Meg said she wanted to make phone calls from the car?

"So," her sister crowed in her obnoxious, singsong voice that was far too loud, "Taylor and I have been talking all about the East Coast."

"Oh yeah?" Kimmie asked. "You have family there or something?"

Meg let out a giggle. "That's where he's from, silly." At least she didn't revert back to her favorite childhood taunt by adding *don't you remember*, but her tone and the expression on her face said the exact same thing.

"I worked on a police force in Massachusetts, but the suburbs felt claustrophobic."

"That's why you moved to Alaska?" Kimmie asked.

Meg nudged him again. "That wasn't the only reason." She batted her eyes as if fleas were threatening to land on her eyeballs.

Taylor looked pensive. "Well, that was one of the reasons."

Kimmie waited for more, hating to imagine there were things about Taylor's life her sister knew that she didn't. She might have asked him for further details, but a woman in a lab coat called his name, and he stood up to walk to the counter.

"What kind of medicine do you think he's on?" Meg whispered as soon as his back was turned.

Meg wasn't talking nearly as quietly as she probably thought, but as humiliating as her question was, Kimmie was simultaneously grateful to learn that Taylor hadn't told her sister everything.

Holding a paper bag with a receipt stapled to the top, Taylor gave a little wave. "It was nice running into you," he said, and this time Kimmie was certain all his attention was focused on Meg. It was just like her sister to monopolize the spotlight, just like she always had.

Meg wiggled her fingers in a playful goodbye, but Kimmie grimaced at the sound of her sister's fake fingernails clanking against each other.

She watched Taylor step toward the exit, still wondering what he had in his paper bag. "See you tonight," she mumbled.

As soon as he was out of the lobby, Meg elbowed her in the side. "You're lucky I'm married, or I would totally be all over that."

Kimmie rolled her eyes. With as shamelessly as Meg acted, nobody would suspect she was married if it weren't for that huge rock on her left hand.

"You really should try to find out what kind of pills he's on," Meg whispered.

Kimmie crossed her arms and waited for Pip's medicine.

CHAPTER 36

"Oh my goodness," Meg squealed as she slid her trim and athletic frame behind the steering wheel. "I still can't get over how cute that trooper is. Did you see those shoulders of his? And he knows how to dress the part, too. Alaska casual looks really good on a man that sculpted."

Kimmie buckled Pip in the back and wondered if now was the right time to remind Meg about her husband in Anchorage.

Sitting down in the passenger side, Kimmie sighed. The PA, unfriendly as she'd been, had ordered antibiotics that should help Pip feel better by the end of the day. He needed one dose now and another at bedtime, but since Kimmie didn't want to do anything to upset his stomach, she decided to wait until he'd had some breakfast.

Meg made a quick stop to Puck's grocery store, and while Kimmie was waiting for her sister, she turned around to glance at Pip. "You hanging in there, Buster?"

Pip refused to look at her. What was wrong? Did he miss

Mom? Was he mad at her for not paying attention to him now that Meg was here hogging all the conversation? She still had that brochure from the PA, along with Tabitha's stinging words. *Shrinking window of opportunity.*

She shouldn't feel guilty. It wasn't like Chuck was a reasonable kind of father who would permit his son to get regular therapy, especially since he assumed Pip was stupid and wasn't worth teaching anyway. The problem was that Kimmie hadn't even tried. She should have at least done what she could to change Chuck's mind. She should have died trying. Now even if Pip started receiving intervention services once they got settled in Anchorage, he might never catch up to where he would have been. She thought back over every interaction with her stepfather, every terrible hungover morning and late drunken evening. There must have been some point in time when she could have brought it up.

Either that or she could have convinced Mom to leave him. Meg managed to change Mom's mind, however surprising it was to think about. Strange that Kimmie and her sister had talked about naturopaths and the immune system and Meg's obsession over Taylor, but they hadn't even talked about what evidence Meg had to show the troopers that Mom was planning to leave.

The evidence that proved Chuck's guilt.

She hated thinking about him, hated the way that even his memory made her skittish. She locked the car doors then felt like a baby. Did she really think Chuck would come here and hurt her or Pip in broad daylight in the middle of a grocery store parking lot?

The truth was she did.

And she was scared.

She turned around in her seat. "You're being such a good traveling buddy." Pip looked tired, and she hoped that after he got a little bit of breakfast and his first dose of medicine he'd nap for most of the trip. He had a lot of sleep to catch up on. She also hoped Meg wasn't going to spend the entire drive to Anchorage lecturing her on the deplorable evils of antibiotics, but it would be just like her. Meg, who never had a kid because she refused to ruin her figure.

Meg came back to the car carrying groceries loose in her arms.

"Did they run out of bags?" Kimmie asked.

Her sister shook her head. "No, but I never use plastic, and I didn't bring my cloth shopping bag in with me."

Kimmie didn't respond.

"I got him some yogurt," Meg said. "Does he like yogurt?"

Kimmie found herself wishing that Meg would ask Pip herself but instead just answered, "He likes it." She took the container from her sister and popped open the door of the backseat. "You hungry, buddy?"

Pip reached out for the yogurt, a good sign.

"Got a spoon?" Kimmie asked.

"I knew I forgot something," Meg exclaimed. "I'll go back in. I need a drink too."

While she waited, Kimmie pulled the antibiotics out of the paper bag she'd gotten at the pharmacy. "All right, Buster. Let's get you healthy again." She shook the bottle, and Pip eyed her warily as she filled the syringe with the chalky white liquid.

Kimmie studied her brother strapped into his toddler seat and decided she'd need to better angle herself. She stepped out of her seat then opened the back door of the car, trying to find the position that would get her closest to her brother while still offering the most protection from his feet and fists if he refused the medicine.

"This is going to make you feel lots better." She heard the trepidation in her own voice and prayed Pip wouldn't throw a fit. She glanced up at his tight lips and knew she was in for a battle.

"Please, Pip, just take this little bit for me, okay?" Her voice turned whiney, but not even her pleading could convince her brother to open his mouth for the syringe.

She lowered herself closer, getting kneed in the chest a few times until she managed to use her body weight to pin his legs against the seat. He gave a loud shriek in protest.

"Please, just take the medicine," she begged.

A woman walked by, and Kimmie wished the car door was shut. The last thing she needed was for some stranger to assume she was abusing her brother and call the troopers. Trying to shush his shouts, she reached out with one hand to try to keep Pip's arms from flailing and held the syringe with her other. Pip's limbs were secured, but he squirmed so much it took all her focus just to keep him pinned down without hurting him.

She wanted to yell even louder than he was, but that would only intensify Pip's reaction. He thrashed his head from side to side, colliding with Kimmie's nose.

"Ouch!" she roared. Tears of frustration threatened to spill out of her eyes. "Just take the stupid medicine." She shoved the syringe into his clamped lips, unsure how much of the liquid was actually going in his mouth and how much had sprayed out over them both. She was breathing heavily when she released his arms and legs. The woman who'd passed her earlier was standing on the sidewalk glaring at them. Kimmie lowered her gaze. She wanted to find a way to explain, to let this stranger know she would never intentionally hurt her brother. But he needed the medicine if he was going to get better, even if his screams made it sound like she was trying to murder him.

She pictured herself forced to repeat the same routine twice a day for a whole week. Why couldn't Pip understand she was trying to help? Kimmie smoothed her hair into place, gave the nosy woman what she hoped was a friendly wave, and got back into her seat.

Meg arrived back at the car, bouncy and breathless. "Got the spoon." She tossed it to the backseat, and Kimmie had to turn around one more time to help Pip open his yogurt container and eat his breakfast. "Does he like that flavor?" Meg asked.

"Yeah. Thank you."

"Well, I figured that since he's going on antibiotics" — she spoke the word as if it were a medieval curse — "we may as well try to build up his digestive tract with as many probiotics as possible. I got him a kombucha too. Does he drink those?"

"I've never heard of it."

Meg shrugged. "Well, it's super good for you. But you might want to check. It could be slightly alcoholic. Hmm. Didn't think about that. I guess maybe you shouldn't give it to him after all. Do you drink coffee?" She handed Kimmie a steaming Kaladi Brothers cup, which she grabbed gratefully.

"Here's some creamers." Meg tossed a few packets into Kimmie's lap. "I have no idea how you take it." She spoke the words spitefully, as if it were Kimmie's fault Meg was never around.

They pulled out of the driveway, and Meg checked the time. "Hmm. I think I probably better cancel that hair appointment after all. Siri, call Denise."

Kimmie crossed her arms while Meg held a conversation with her cell phone and then with her stylist. Wasn't Meg going to take care of that at the clinic? Oh, well. Ninety percent of what Meg did Kimmie would never understand. Like how she could stand to live with a man whose only ambition was to sell houses and have the most bleached blond hair and darkest tan in Anchorage.

Or how she'd finally convinced Mom to find the courage to leave Chuck.

Once they got back on the Glenn, Kimmie turned around in her seat, checking every so often until Pip fell asleep. After his eyes closed, she waited a little longer just to be sure then faced her sister.

"All right," she said. "I want to hear about Mom, and I want you to tell me everything."

CHAPTER 37

For a woman who had always exuded confidence and haughtiness, Meg seemed the slightest bit uncertain. "Are you sure you want to get into all this now?"

Kimmie crossed her arms. "I'm sure."

"Really? Because I know you had a hard night last night, and you probably still need to catch up on your rest. Why don't you take a nap first or something?"

"I just had all that coffee. Now tell me. You and Mom made plans for her to escape. That's what you told Taylor."

"Who?"

Kimmie rolled her eyes. Really? For as long as Meg had been flirting with the trooper after setting him up on a forced date, she had already forgotten his name?

Typical.

"Taylor," she repeated with emphasis. "The trooper."

Meg grinned. "Oh, yeah. Him. I still think you need to find out what meds he's taking before you let things get too serious.

184

But he's crazy hot. I'll admit that. I could totally see the two of you together."

Then why in the world did you have your paws all over him? Kimmie wanted to yell, but she held her tongue. She wasn't charging into this conversation to get news about Taylor. She needed to hear about Mom.

Now.

"What happened? What haven't you told me?"

Meg took in a deep breath. "Well, I can tell you, but I still think you should rest a little bit and we can talk when you're feeling a little better. I could wake you up once we get to Eureka ..."

"Just get it over with," Kimmie snapped.

"Fine." Meg was clearly annoyed and saw no need to hide it. "Mom called me a couple weeks ago. Asked if I knew of any good lawyers, someone who could help her fight for custody of Pip. I told her Dwayne's got connections. We could figure something out."

"How did she even get in touch with you?" Kimmie asked.

"On her cell. The one I got her last Christmas."

"Mom had a cell?" For a minute, Kimmie wondered if they'd stopped talking about the same person.

"Yeah. I'm surprised she didn't tell you."

Apparently, there were plenty of things Mom hadn't told her. Kimmie found herself yet again facing pangs of jealousy when she thought about her sister and the secret conversations she had with their mom.

"I thought you two were still fighting over Chuck."

Meg waved her hand in the air dismissively. Kimmie wished she'd keep it on the wheel. "What, that? Water under the bridge. We talked once or twice a week. Even more once I got her that phone."

None of it made sense. "When did she find a way to call you? Where did she go to get reception?"

"You really haven't been keeping up with the times, have you?"

Kimmie blinked at her sister.

"Coverage isn't what it was three or five years ago. The whole trailer's a hot spot. Mom even got herself a Facebook account. Used it on her phone all the time."

"What? You're serious?"

Meg chuckled. "I know. It was ridiculous, someone her age learning Facebook. But it was adorable, I swear."

"Why didn't she tell me any of this?"

"She probably didn't want you to get in trouble with that jerkface she was with. Oh, by the way, is the kid asleep?"

Kimmie glanced back again. "Yeah, he started dozing off right after we passed Mendeltna."

Meg let out her breath. "Good. I mean, I know he doesn't talk and all, but I'd hate to have him hear what I've got to say about his dad."

"You can skip that part," Kimmie said curtly. "I'm pretty sure I know more about that than you."

"Right. Well, so I got Mom that cell phone at Christmas ..."

"What'd you do?" Kimmie interrupted. "Hide it in the fruitcake?"

Meg looked appalled. "No. I told her I'd left it with Mrs. Spencer next door."

"Mrs. Spencer knew Mom had a cell phone?" Kimmie thought back to all the times she'd trekked to her neighbor's house to make a call. What kind of dysfunctional family did Mrs. Spencer think she was living next to?

"You're missing the point," Meg complained. "The point is once Mom got her phone, she and I were able to stay in touch. She'd call me whenever Bozohead was taking a nap, and that's how I found out just how bad things were."

Kimmie stared out the window at the mountains in the distance. Right now, their snow-dusted peaks felt closer to her than either her sister or her mom.

"Hey, it's not like she wanted to keep secrets from you." Meg sounded defensive. "You know how things were at that home. Everyone had to keep everything from everybody. That's just the way it was for you guys."

For you guys. Kimmie wondered how easy it was for her sister to throw around those kinds of phrases. *For you guys.*

Apparently taking Kimmie's silence for further offense, Meg ran her hand through her hair and huffed. "It's not like it was easy for me either, Cinderella. You think I liked to hear about the things that creature was doing to you?"

Kimmie bristled. Whatever happened to her under Chuck's roof wasn't her sister's business. And the fact that Mom blabbed everything to such a snotty, stuck-up, plastic Barbie doll like Meg doubled the sense of betrayal.

"Finally, Mom called me and said she wanted my help getting away."

Kimmie bet Meg just loved that. The chance for her big sister with the huge bank account and just as massive messiah complex to whisk in and save her wretched family from the clutches of evil. How grandiose. It must have given Meg quite the rush to be involved in anything more important than filing papers for her snotty husband.

"Why are you glaring at me like that?" Meg finally

demanded.

"I'm not glaring." Kimmie glowered out the window.

"Yes, you are. You asked me a question. Now I'm telling you the answer, and you're acting all hurt and depressed. It's not like it's something I like to talk about."

"You certainly had no problems telling everything to that trooper," Kimmie blurted.

"So that's what this is about?" Meg had a bad habit of flaring her nostrils when she got angry, one of her only physically unattractive qualities. Kimmie reveled to see that her picture-perfect sister wasn't quite as put together as she wanted everyone to believe. "Listen, if you're upset because I went to the authorities to get you the help you obviously needed ..."

"I'm upset because you never cared!" Kimmie raised her voice, surrendering to the anger that gave her entire psyche a sense of power she'd rarely felt before. "You never cared. You ran off as soon as Mom got together with Chuck, and you never looked back."

Meg swerved to avoid hitting two ravens pecking at roadkill in the middle of their lane. "Is that what you think happened?" Her nostrils flared even more wildly.

"That's not what I think happened. That's what I know happened."

Each time Meg spoke, her volume escalated. "You know nothing. Hear me? I died when I found out what that oaf was doing to Mom. I literally died. Want me to prove it?"

She yanked up her sleeve. "See? That's what I did when I heard. By the time Dwayne called the paramedics, I didn't have a pulse. So don't even think about talking to me about who's suffered more or who put up with what or who hurts the most now that Mom's gone. Because you don't even know the half of it."

Meg gasped for breath as tears rolled down her cheeks. For what felt like minutes, Kimmie was too stunned to say a word. Finally, she forced herself to open the glove compartment where she found a travel packet of Kleenex. She pulled one out and offered it to her sister as a gesture of goodwill.

"Thanks." Meg blew her nose loudly then dabbed at her eyes. "I knew I shouldn't have put on all that mascara." She choked out a laugh. Kimmie joined in, feeling even more awkward and embarrassed than she'd been the day when she was ten and got caught trying on her sister's pushup bra.

"Mom never told me," Kimmie finally confessed.

Meg shrugged. "Of course she didn't. She never knew."

Kimmie didn't know what else to say. Staring at the snow capping the mountains ahead, she imagined how lonely and isolated it would feel to be up there looking down at a single car edging its way down a deserted highway.

The termination dust glistened in the sunlight.

CHAPTER 38

Kimmie woke up when the car rolled to a stop. "Where are we?"

"Just past the air force base," Meg answered. "Looks like you got bored playing Cinderella and tried to be Sleeping Beauty for the day."

Kimmie wasn't amused at her sister's little joke. She must have crashed shortly after their fight about Mom because she didn't remember anything else from the drive.

"Has Pip been napping this whole time?" She turned around as best she could in her seat.

"He's fine. Poor kid needs his sleep."

Kimmie glanced at her sister and whispered, "Sorry."

Meg shrugged. "Me, too."

Kimmie wanted to say more. Needed to say more. She still didn't know the details of Mom's escape or anything else Meg had talked with the trooper about.

"We'll be home in a half an hour. Maybe a little less if

192

traffic stays this light."

It had been years since Kimmie's last trip to Anchorage. Pip had never been to a city this size, and she wondered if he'd be mesmerized by the traffic and crowds or terrified. She should warn Meg. Find a way to tell her about how Pip could freak out if too many changes were introduced at once. Maybe this move had been a bad idea after all. Then again, it's not like they could have stayed in Glennallen. So much had happened since yesterday, she realized she hadn't even called Jade to tell her she wasn't coming in to the daycare.

She winced in disapproval. "I can't believe it."

"What's wrong?" her sister asked.

"I missed my shift at work. I didn't let anybody know I wouldn't be able to make it."

Meg tossed her hair over her shoulder. "I'm sure everyone will understand once you tell them about last night."

"Yeah, but I don't even have their phone number," Kimmie whined. Compared to nearly losing her brother to hypothermia and getting lost with him in the woods escaping from a murderous stepfather, missing work was a relatively minor burden, but she'd never flaked out like that before. She shook her head. "Jade's going to hate me."

"Jade?" Meg repeated. "Is that the one whose phone you

were borrowing the other day?"

"Yeah."

"Then her number's still in my cell. You can call her and save your conscience." She tossed the phone onto Kimmie's lap. "Here you go. Have at it."

Kimmie tried a few times but wasn't even sure how to turn it on.

"Wait," Meg huffed, then softened her voice to add, "Let me do it."

"Can you do that while you're driving?" Kimmie asked when her sister took her phone back.

"Of course I can. It's not like I'm dialing or anything." She held the phone close to her mouth. "Siri, open recent calls."

Her request was met with a mechanical beep as the phone lit up.

Meg passed it over. "Just find the one from yesterday and hit that green phone icon."

Kimmie still couldn't get her mind around her own mother having a contraption this fancy. All those months and Chuck never found out? A second later, Jade was on the line, and Kimmie gave her the very abbreviated rundown of why she had to leave town.

"Everything okay?" Meg asked when Kimmie ended the

call.

"Yeah," she answered, feeling sheepish for being so worried earlier. "I guess strep's going around the whole daycare, so Jade's only got four kids in today anyway. She's doing fine."

Meg didn't say *I told you so,* but her smug smile spoke volumes.

"Now that we're back in civilization, mind if I turn the radio on?" Meg reached out toward the dial. Soon her loud, booming music stole any further chance Kimmie had to ask her more about their mom. Unfortunately, the noise didn't manage to drown out her feelings of confusion and fear.

CHAPTER 39

Mom had bragged about Meg's house, but Kimmie had thought she'd been exaggerating until they pulled up into the winding driveway. At one point, Meg had to stop and put in a code that automatically opened a heavy brass gate. To the right was a tiered landscape with shrubs and mulch that looked as fresh as if it had just been poured out of the bag. To the left were tall brick pillars every few feet covered in some kind of lavish ivy.

"This driveway must take the entire day just to shovel in the winter," she commented.

It wasn't until her sister started to laugh that Kimmie realized Meg and her husband would pay someone to plow any snow that accumulated in front of their house.

Meg pushed the button on her sun visor that opened an immaculate garage, cleaner than the interior of most people's houses. A few garden tools with matching pink handles hung on one wall, bikes and tennis equipment on another. A golf bag in the corner was the only item that wasn't hung or somehow suspended above the perfectly swept concrete floor.

"Come on in." Meg stepped out of the car and tilted up her chin, probably waiting for Kimmie's gushing words of praise. The problem was Kimmie couldn't even find her voice.

"Wake up, Pip." Kimmie wondered if he was going to spend the whole day sleeping. Was it normal for him to be this tired? She shouldn't overreact. He was going to be fine. Everything was going to be fine.

She thought about the ornate gate with its automated code. She didn't even know people had homes like this in Anchorage but was thankful for the extra security it would afford. For the first time since her mom died, she wondered if things were actually going to start getting better.

"Take off your shoes," Meg called behind her shoulder as she stepped into a kitchen with massive windows and a vaulted sky roof. She turned around, beaming, but Kimmie still had no idea what she was supposed to say.

"Wow," she stammered, which was apparently enough to loosen Meg's tongue.

"Dwayne designed this place as an early wedding gift for the two of us. He told me I could either have the skylight in the ceiling or a honeymoon in Greece, and then when I told him I just couldn't make up my mind, he surprised me and gave me both." Her giggle was even more grating and airy than usual.

"Sweet cakes, is that you?" A tan Ken doll lookalike stepped into the kitchen and gave Meg a kiss on the cheek. "I didn't know you were bringing company over." He stretched out his hand. "Hi. I'm Dwayne."

Kimmie blinked at him, surprised to find that he looked exactly like he did in the wedding picture Mom had hanging on the fridge back home, right down to the last pixel. She was also surprised that he didn't seem to know who she was.

"Kimberly," she told him as she shook his hand.

"Nice to meet you, Kimberly. It's always lovely meeting one of my bride's friends."

Kimmie glanced at her sister who swatted him playfully with her handbag. "Bunny-boo, this is my *sister.*"

Dwayne's eyes widened. *"You're* Kimmie?"

Meg laughed, but not convincingly enough to keep Kimmie from picking up on the slightly nervous edge. "I told you she might be coming here to stay for a little while."

"Oh, great." Dwayne's smile hadn't changed once since he stepped into the room. Kimmie wondered how he managed without giving his cheeks some massive cramps. He bent down to kiss his wife again, whispering loudly, "She staying in the upstairs guest room or downstairs?"

"Downstairs," Meg answered just as conspiratorially.

Dwayne nodded. "Well, I'm off."

"Where you going, baby-bear?" Meg asked with an exaggerated pout.

"Work, work, work." He stuck out his finger and pressed in Meg's petite button nose.

"Boop!" she responded with a giggle, and after a fair amount of nose-kissing, cooing, and name-calling, he was gone.

Meg let out one last laugh when he left. "So that was Dwayne."

Kimmie hadn't realized until she saw her sister relax that Meg's smile had been just as huge and just as unwavering as her husband's during their entire exchange. Her sister sank down onto one of the tall barstools around a marble island countertop, moaning something about being too early in the day for wine.

"Can I do anything to help around the house?" Kimmie stared at the immaculate kitchen, wondering how her sister managed to keep herself from getting lost in her own home.

Her words seemed to sweep away whatever exhaustion cloud had covered her sister. Meg lifted up her head. "No, no, everything's taken care of here. Come on. Let me show you to your new room."

CHAPTER 40

"Sorry," Meg said, staring at the sparse bedroom. "I really had no idea what kind of toys a typical three-year-old would play with, and even if I did, I wasn't sure what would be appropriate for Pip."

Kimmie tried not to let her annoyance show. Meg was trying. The two women hadn't fought since their spat in the car, but every sentence felt strained. Like they both knew this was some kind of an act, but even the stress of keeping up such a complicated pretense was easier to deal with than the bickering and jealousy that had polluted their relationship for years.

Meg had already given them a tour of the house, explaining which rooms Dwayne considered on and off limits. Kimmie figured if she stuck with the guest room, the attached bathroom, and the kitchen, she'd be perfectly safe. She didn't even know where Meg and her husband slept.

Kimmie watched her sister shuffle from one foot to the other and felt a little bit sorry for her. It wasn't her fault that she was trying so hard to impress them.

"Any idea how you want to spend the rest of your afternoon?" Meg asked. "We could take Pip out for lunch and go to the park."

Kimmie wondered if Meg remembered the playground Mom used to take them to a lifetime ago. "Is there still that playground with the giant jungle gym?"

Meg frowned. "Which one do you mean? The one on Tudor and Lake Otis?"

"It was red and green and blue, and it had a swing coming down from the center and games like tic-tac-toe and stuff you could play on the sides."

Meg shook her head. "I don't remember any like that, but I know a nice one with a little foot bridge and a stream. It's getting cold, but the ducks were still there the last time I drove by. Does Pip like feeding ducks?"

Kimmie wished her sister would stop asking questions like that. Didn't she understand that for his entire life, Pip's existence had been relegated to his bedroom and the daycare? The only playground he'd ever known was the cheap plastic one at work. It was small, only room for two or three at a time, and other than a two-week period where he decided he loved the swings, Pip had never shown any interest in it at all.

"Let's not worry about a park today," Kimmie decided. Pip didn't act like his throat hurt, but she figured it was still too soon to take him out for a lot of running around.

"You sure? I could ask some of my mom friends. They might know of one with a jungle gym. Does he like to climb or something? Maybe we could set up a playdate."

Kimmie shook her head. The last thing she wanted to do was sit with dozens of other kids whose obvious developmental advancements just made Pip's delays seem even more exaggerated. And since he'd just gotten diagnosed with strep, she doubted parents would want him around their kids either.

"I think that we just need some downtime for a while. Is that all right with you?" She wasn't used to tiptoeing around her sister's feelings, but she asked the question gently, uncertain exactly what it was that she was trying to protect Meg from.

Meg nodded. "That sounds good. Does he have a favorite movie? We've got Netflix and Amazon and Hulu if there's something he wants to stream."

"Let me get him settled in for a little bit," Kimmie said even though she and Pip didn't have a single bag of personal belongings between them. She'd probably have to ask Meg to take her shopping soon, an excursion her sister would adore and Kimmie despise. But right now, she needed a few minutes alone. A few minutes with her thoughts and with her brother without anyone else staring over her shoulder or worrying about her.

She offered Meg an unconvincing smile. "It's going to be all right," she promised. "I just think Pip needs a little bit of quiet, and then we can decide what to do with the rest of the day."

"Okay." Meg lifted her hand and gave a little wave before shutting the door behind them, and Kimmie spent the next several minutes staring at the flowered wallpaper in silence.

CHAPTER 41

Meg came home with Subway sandwiches a little over an hour later.

"It doesn't look like that fever's done much to suppress his appetite, does it?" Meg asked, glancing at Pip.

Kimmie hadn't seen her brother eat so much before in a single sitting. Then again, between the rationed meals at the daycare and Chuck's bread heels and chili leftovers, this may have been the first chance Pip ever had to eat however much he wanted. How sad would it be to learn that all of his delays were simply a symptom of malnourishment? Then again, maybe that would be good news because his body and brain would catch up as soon as he got the calories and nutrients he'd been denied for so long.

It was nearly impossible for Kimmie to keep up any sort of conversation while they ate. She wanted to ask Meg more about their mom, but she'd have to wait for a time when Pip wasn't within earshot. Given how long he'd slept in the car, Kimmie doubted he'd take his regular afternoon nap. His schedule, his whole life, was thrown off balance, and she was both surprised and grateful he hadn't started throwing fits yet. Maybe that was another symptom of the strep. Maybe he was too tired to act up.

"So, work's going well for Dwayne?" Kimmie asked after an awkward silence.

Meg took a bite of her vegan wrap and shrugged. "You'd have to ask him. It's not like he talks to me about any of it."

"I thought you were his assistant or something."

Meg shrugged again. "Just because you work for somebody doesn't mean you know what they're up to." Her words were strangely cryptic and her expression somber enough that Kimmie tried to think of some way to change the subject.

"You sure it'll be okay for Taylor and me to have dinner here tonight? That won't be weird since you'll be out?"

Meg laughed. "What, are you young enough that you still need a chaperone on a date? Or are you worried about being alone with someone who's on prescription meds and you don't know what they are?"

Kimmie felt herself blush and tried to hide her face behind her sub. "Will you get off his stupid prescription?"

"Fine. Then you tell me why you all of a sudden want to back out on a date with Alaska's most eligible trooper."

Kimmie rolled her eyes before taking a bite. "I just wanted to make sure it's not weird for you or anything."

"Not at all. I think it's adorable. You should've heard all the questions he was asking about you when you and Pip were with the doctor. I think he really likes you."

"You're just saying that." Kimmie tried to ignore the heat in her cheeks and the fluttering of her heart.

"No, I'm not. He asked all kinds of things. If you had a boyfriend, what kind of guys you typically date."

"What did you tell him?"

"The truth, of course. I told him that you only date guys with hard, chiseled jawlines, trim and athletic physiques, and that you once told me there was nothing in the world sexier than a man in uniform."

Kimmie stared at her sister, too mortified to speak.

Meg chuckled and took a sip of her bottled water. "Don't worry. I didn't really say all that. Although I might've mentioned something about uniforms."

Kimmie wasn't sure if Meg was still joking and decided that it might be better if she let the subject drop.

"I'm really happy for you," Meg finally said. "He seems like a decent guy, and he obviously cares about you and Pip. Even if he is on meds." Kimmie finished her sandwich in silence.

After lunch, Meg turned on the Pixar movie *Cars* for Pip. It was one of the ones he had already seen and seemed somewhat interested in at the daycare. Kimmie figured that with everything else going on right now, anything she could do to surround him with the familiar would be beneficial.

Once he was settled comfortably in the living room, Kimmie and Meg sat at the tall kitchen barstools and started brainstorming a shopping list.

"I have tons of clothes that you can have, so other than socks and underwear, I think you'll be set. What about shoes? If you're still a seven, mine will be a little big for you."

Kimmie glanced down at her feet. "I just brought my tennis shoes, and that will be fine for now." She didn't want to think about the approaching winter, the fact that before long she'd need snow boots and hats and gloves. She thought about one of mom's favorite Bible verses. *Do not worry about tomorrow, for tomorrow will worry about itself.* If God could get all of the Alaskan plants and animals and wildlife ready for winter, he could do the same thing for her too.

With Pip, on the other hand, it would be a little trickier not to worry.

"My friend Shannon's got a boy who just turned four, and

she's not planning on having any more kids, so she's going to bring a few big bags of clothes, but she can't come until tomorrow. Do you want me to pick him up an outfit or two to wear until then? And what about pajamas?"

Kimmie didn't mention that with as difficult as it was to make it to the laundromat, Pip usually wore the same clothes several days in a row.

"I think he'll be fine until then, but I guess if you find any dinosaur pajamas, he really liked his pair from back home." She ignored the tightening in her throat when she thought about everything her brother was forced to leave behind. "They were green," she added quietly.

Meg gave her a sympathetic glance, and for a moment Kimmie worried that the dam she'd erected around her emotions since her mom's death was about to break. She would tell Meg everything, all about those years of torment, the shame and fear that now felt just as much a part of her as her DNA. She wanted to cry, to tell her sister how much she missed Mom, how impossible it was to think that someone so loving could kill herself or end up murdered.

She wanted to asked Meg what she thought about their time together as children. Was she disappointed that they had drifted so far apart? Did she secretly hope that this time of living under

209

the same roof might be the first step toward healing that giant rift that had come between them?

Instead, she rattled off some of the toiletries she and Pip might need.

"Seriously?" Meg looked at the list she'd just written. "That's all you want me to get? Just toothbrushes, toothpaste, and a hairbrush?"

Kimmie stared at her lap. If she asked for more, she was afraid of overtaxing her sister's generosity. If she stuck with this list of the bare necessities, though, Meg might feel insulted as a hostess.

Maybe sensing Kimmie's discomfort, Meg smiled. "I guess you're right. Our skin tones are so close to the same that whatever I use for makeup I'm sure will work for you too. What about snacks? Dwayne and I are so busy we usually eat out or just pick up some takeout on our way home from the office. With Pip not feeling good though, I thought maybe I could get a few snacks and some easy breakfast stuff just to keep on hand. Should I get more yogurt?"

"Yes, please," Kimmie answered, once again feeling overwhelmed by this display of opulence, privilege, and generosity.

"What about for breakfast? You know me. I'm no cook, but

I could grab something easy. Does he have a favorite cereal? Does he like granola? Hey." Meg reached out her hand and gave Kimmie's shoulder a squeeze. "What's wrong? Did I say something?"

Kimmie sniffed and wiped the tears from her eyes.

"What's the matter?" Meg asked the question so directly that Kimmie didn't have time to think up a lie.

"I don't know what he likes to eat for breakfast."

Her sister stared at her blankly. Of course it wouldn't make sense to someone like Meg, someone who could eat out or call for delivery or hop in her fancy car and drive to any grocery store or restaurant she wanted. Meg would never know what it was like to be so poor that a single crust of bread would be split between three people. She and Meg were born and raised by the same woman, but they were from completely different universes. Today was the first time Pip ever had a choice about what he ate, which only made the fact that he couldn't talk even more heart wrenching.

Kimmie sniffed. "I'm all right. It's just been a long day."

Meg looked at her quizzically, her pen still hovering over her pad of paper. "So, something simple like Cheerios, maybe?"

Kimmie sunk her head into her hands, wondering how something as simple as making a shopping list grew to be so draining. "Yeah," she answered, finding each word laborious to croak out. "Cheerios sound fine."

CHAPTER 42

Kimmie lost track of how many times she'd checked in on Pip in the living room while Meg was out shopping. The moment her sister said goodbye, Kimmie realized she should have asked Meg to pick up a few cheap matchbox cars, but she felt too silly to chase her down in the garage and add one more item to her list.

Kimmie had no idea what Pip could do here to occupy his time besides watching movies, but they'd think of something. Anchorage wasn't quite as cold as Glennallen. Maybe she and her brother could spend some time outside. The neighborhood was quiet. Kimmie could get used to living here.

If she had to.

Hopefully, the arrangement would be temporary. As soon as Kimmie found a job, she'd start looking for a place of her own. Meg's house felt more like a museum on display than a home where a kid would be free to run and jump and play. If Pip ever did any of those things.

She'd felt her brother's forehead on at least five different occasions in the past hour. How long was Meg going to take grabbing a few snacks and toiletries? Then again, Anchorage wasn't like Glennallen with its one grocery store. From Meg's home, it took at least a quarter of an hour just to get off the hillside. Driving to downtown Anchorage would probably take an hour if you ran into traffic.

But there were advantages to living in a city, advantages that Kimmie was prepared to seize. On the drive to her sister's, they'd passed two different storefronts with speech therapy signs. Pip would be in good hands. And hopefully Kimmie would find a job soon.

A door slammed. Kimmie turned around. "Hello?"

She checked the garage, but her sister wasn't home yet.

"Is someone here?" She hurried to the living room, where Pip was wrapped in blankets watching *Cars*. She checked his forehead once again out of habit. At least his fever was going down. "Do you need anything, Buster?" she asked. "Do you have to use the bathroom?" She glanced around, wondering if he'd wandered off in search of a toilet, but from what she could tell, he hadn't moved since the last time she checked on him.

Maybe she was hearing things.

She eyed the front door. It was still locked. Which was

generally a good sign, but only if you weren't trapped in a house with doors that closed on their own.

And a floor that creaked like someone was walking right behind her.

"Dwayne?" Kimmie's voice was shaky and uncertain. Even if someone had been in the next room, they probably wouldn't have heard her. She peeked out the front window to see if there were any cars in the driveway. But how could anyone get past that big iron gate?

Another sound, this one from the level above. Something moved upstairs. Suddenly, Kimmie's lungs started to seize up. What if it was Chuck? How hard would it be to find Meg's home address? He knew where Kimmie was, and he was coming after her. That had to be it.

She shoved her hand into her pants pocket, where Taylor's business card was crumpled from all the times she'd handled it. She had no idea what kind of long-distance rates Meg got on her landline, but whatever it was, she and Dwayne could afford it. Kimmie hurried to the kitchen, and her fingers shook while she dialed the number.

"Hello, this is Taylor." He sounded so casual. So happy.

She wet her lips and tried to steady her voice. "Hi. It's Kimmie. I'm at my sister's."

"Oh, yeah." From his jocular tone, Kimmie could almost see Taylor's warm smile. "You calling to give me her address? I'm on the road still, so I won't be able to write it down."

Kimmie's neck tingled with the vague sense she was being watched. She lowered her voice and took the phone closer to the hallway where she could keep an eye on her brother. Pip hadn't moved. So what was making all that noise?

"Kimmie? You still there?"

"Yeah," she whispered.

Taylor chuckled. "Good. I thought you had cut out on me for a minute. Reception's not great around here. Mind if I call you back in a little bit? We're about an hour still from the airport."

"I think someone's in the house."

Taylor paused, and when he spoke his voice was deadly serious. "You're at your sister's?"

"Yeah. She went to get some groceries, but I think I heard a noise upstairs."

A staticky noise garbled his words when he asked, "What kind of noise?"

"A door shutting. Someone making the floor creak." She held her breath, waiting for Taylor to tell her that all Anchorage mansions creaked, that they all had drafts that could blow doors

216

shut unexpectedly. She wished she could look at him right now, wished she could borrow a little of the strength she always managed to find when he was nearby.

"Given everything you've gone through, you can't be too careful," he said, his voice taking on a mechanical quality. "I think you should ..." His next words were even more garbled.

"What?" She gripped the phone, straining to make sense of his words through the static. "Taylor? Are you there?"

Her sister's phone beeped in her ear. She'd lost the call.

CHAPTER 43

Kimmie stared alternatively at her brother and the phone in her hand. What should she do? She tried calling her sister's cell, but it went straight to voicemail. In a way, she was glad. She didn't want Meg to see her freaking out like this.

Every house made noise. She glanced out the window. The trees at the back of Meg's property swayed their branches grandly. It was probably just the wind.

Kimmie glanced around, wondering where she could take Pip if they needed to lock themselves in somewhere. The thought was silly. She was free now. Chuck had no idea where she was. Besides, there were troopers looking for him all around Glennallen. He couldn't have made it all the way to Anchorage, could he? She doubted his truck would even run that far.

No, it wasn't Chuck, and she didn't need to rush into a closet with Pip and hide. She was an adult who was acting like a child staying home alone for the first time. She marched back to the kitchen, listening at the same spot where she'd heard the door slam earlier. Nothing. The wind or her imagination. That was all. She glanced down the hallway and up the carpeted stairs leading to the second story. What could stop her from checking things out, just to be safe? She was tired of running, tired of hiding, and tired of being scared. Clutching her sister's phone with one hand, she rummaged through Meg's drawers with the other until she found a large cutting knife.

Nobody would catch her unprepared. Because nobody was upstairs. Still, having a weapon gave her a sense of power.

Not that she'd need it.

"I'll be back in a sec," she told her brother as she passed by the living room. He didn't glance up from the TV.

Tiptoeing up the stairs, Kimmie steadied her breath. She was going to confront her fears head-on this time and prove to herself that nobody else could be in this house.

She'd only been upstairs once, and half the doors had remained shut when Meg gave her the grand tour. Should she open each door one at a time to prove to herself that she was alone?

A thumping noise from down the hallway. This time Kimmie was certain of it. She stared at the knife in her hand. What good would it do against armed robbers? What good would it do against Chuck and his rifle?

A whispered voice. More than one person?

She still held the phone, but if she turned it on the beeping noise might alert the intruders. She had to get back down to Pip. Had to get him to safety.

Kimmie strained her ears, expecting almost anything — gunfire, Chuck's angry curses. What she didn't expect was a loud, shrill giggle.

She froze in the hallway, unable to move her legs as the far door opened and her brother-in-law poked his head out. "Kimmie?"

She tried to hide the phone and the knife behind her back but was certain he saw them both. Heat rushed so fast up to her face she felt dizzy. "I didn't know you were home," was all she managed to stammer.

"Just for a minute. I had to grab something I forgot." He cocked his head to the side. "Are you okay?"

Kimmie's hands were sweating so much she was afraid she might drop the knife. "I'm fine. I just heard a noise and got a little startled. That's all."

He smiled at her, but his expression did nothing to dull her sense of fear mingled with mortification.

Kimmie thought she heard another noise coming from the back room, but she wasn't about to step forward and investigate. She turned to head back downstairs when Dwayne called after her. "Hey, Kimmie?"

He'd plastered on that same fake smile he'd worn when they first met. She didn't know why the look should disgust her so much, but it did.

"Yeah?" Why couldn't he leave her to die of humiliation in peace?

"Meg's always getting on me for leaving things at home, so I'd love it if you didn't mention I was here." He winked. "Sorry for scaring you."

She turned away as his door clicked back in place to the sound of a stifled giggle.

CHAPTER 44

Kimmie didn't hear when or if Dwayne left, but the house was quiet when *Cars* ended, and she figured whatever business he'd wanted to get done at home was accomplished. Pip was restless, wandering from room to room. Kimmie followed him mindlessly. What else was there for her to do?

Meg came home a little before five, carrying at least half a dozen fabric shopping bags, which she dumped on the counter before racing upstairs. "I'm so late. I've got to get ready for that thing with Dwayne tonight. Follow me upstairs, and we can talk while I get ready." She rattled off the things she bought, and Kimmie was amazed that her sister could turn a seven-item list into a several-hundred-dollar shopping spree.

"Oh, and I know I said you could wear my clothes, but I saw this cardigan sweater and figured it'd look really good with some black slacks for your date tonight. You'll have to let me know if it fits." Meg tossed it to her and scurried into her bathroom, where she immediately began emptying her drawers haphazardly. "You excited about spending time with that cute trooper? Have you noticed how sexy he sounds when he laughs? You better tell me everything that happens tonight, or I'll totally die of jealousy. By the way, how'd things go while I was gone? Were you bored? Did you figure out how to use the TV remote? Is Pip feeling any better?"

Kimmie glanced at Meg's bed, where Pip had been fingering the raised patterns of her quilt, but he wasn't there anymore. "Pip?"

Kimmie retraced their steps downstairs, her heart high in her throat. Finally, she found Pip pulling a bag with dozens of matchbox cars out of one of Meg's shopping bags.

"Are these cars all for him?" she called up the stairs.

Meg appeared at the top of the landing. "Yeah. I remember Mom mentioned that he liked them."

Kimmie was touched by the gesture and glad that now Pip would have something to do to occupy his time besides wandering from room to room, feeling up the different blankets and pillows and upholsteries. She had to pull the butcher knife back out of the drawer to cut the box open, which reminded her of how scared she'd been when she'd heard her brother-in-law upstairs. She needed to call Taylor too and let him know she was all right. The afternoon had whizzed past.

She carried the new toys upstairs where Pip could play with them in Meg's room, hoping her sister wouldn't mind the mess.

Meg was in front of her mirror, running a flat iron through her hair. "I can't believe it took me that long just to get everything. I hope I'm not late. Dwayne throws a fit about that."

Kimmie still hadn't decided what, if anything, she'd tell her sister about seeing Dwayne at the house. It wasn't her business for one thing, and it would make things awkward for the rest of her stay if she and her brother-in-law started this visit on bad terms. On the other hand, Kimmie was sick of secrets, sick of having to pretend. She had no idea what Dwayne was doing this afternoon at home, and even though she had her suspicions, she doubted Meg would listen even if Kimmie did decide to share.

She'd have time to think through things later. She'd met Dwayne for all of two minutes. She shouldn't jump to conclusions.

Meg brushed her hair into place, pouting until she got it just right. She glanced at Kimmie's reflection in the mirror and asked, "So what time's Officer Cutie coming to dinner?"

"Around six," Kimmie answered. "I still need to call and give him your address."

"Use my cell." Meg pointed to her handbag on the bed. "I already put his name in there."

224

Kimmie was impressed that she managed to get the phone turned on, but after that she was lost.

"Here, give it to me," Meg ordered, then taking the phone said, "Siri, call Taylor's cell." She shoved the phone back to Kimmie when it started ringing.

"Kimmie?" His voice sounded panicked. "I've been really worried about you. I kept trying to dial the number you used to call me earlier, but it went straight to voicemail."

Meg leaned over and called out, "That must have been the landline. I've got the ringer turned off."

Kimmie blushed, realizing she was on speaker, and walked down the hallway where she hoped she could find a little privacy. For all she knew, Dwayne was home again and about to pop out of the room at the far end of the hall.

"Are you all right?" Taylor asked. "I was worried. I almost called the local police to check on you."

"I'm sorry." She should have called him right back, but she was so embarrassed to have let her brother-in-law freak her out that she'd conveniently forgotten. "Did you get your friend to the airport all right?"

"Yeah. You still free for dinner?"

Kimmie thought of all the reasons why Taylor shouldn't come over. She hardly knew him, for one thing, and she didn't like the thought that he was paying her attention just because he was sorry for her. It felt strange and somewhat rude hosting someone at her sister's house, especially with Meg out for the evening. Besides, she had Pip to worry about. What if his fever spiked?

"I hope you like Chinese." Taylor's voice was playful, and Kimmie's arguments died on her lips.

"That sounds delicious."

"Where should I meet you?"

Kimmie stepped back into the bedroom where Meg shouted him her address through her closed closet door while she dressed.

"Did you catch that?" Kimmie asked with a laugh. She nearly tripped over one of Pip's cars as she stepped back out of the room.

"I got it," Taylor answered. "I'll see you pretty soon. And Kimmie?"

"Yeah?" She waited, her heart a fluttering bird in her chest.

"I'm really looking forward to spending some time together."

CHAPTER 45

Aside from Pip's throwing a minor tantrum when Kimmie moved his car collection back downstairs to the living room, the evening went smoothly enough. Meg was a bundle of nerves and motion until she swept out at quarter to six, complaining about how late she'd be, wishing Kimmie good luck on her big date as if it were a final exam at school.

The door slammed shut behind her with an echo, and then the house fell silent. Kimmie had showered and changed into a pair of her sister's black slacks and a black shirt. It was darker than what she'd normally wear, but the burgundy cardigan and a turquoise necklace from her sister gave a cheerful splash of color. She'd lost track of how many times she'd opened and shut the kitchen cabinets just so she could remember where everything was when Taylor arrived with the food.

Pip adored his new dinosaur pajamas from Meg and was already dressed for bed. Kimmie was glad he was happy playing with those cars. Her sister might never know what a genius purchase that was. Kimmie wandered from room to room, wondering what she could do to make anything look more attractive. The house was spotless, and the decorations were sparse but tasteful. She hoped it wasn't too opulent for Taylor. She didn't want to make him uncomfortable, didn't want him to think she came from the kind of family that had nothing better to do than flaunt all their wealth to make others jealous.

She tried to imagine how the night would go. She'd never been on a date before. Even though she and a boy in high school had crushes on each other for a while, she'd never been allowed to see him outside of school. She wondered if Meg was this nervous before her first date with Dwayne.

Kimmie glanced once more at the mirror, hardly recognizing herself. From one angle, she looked tired and old, like you'd expect from someone who'd just lost their mother. But when the light caught her face a certain way and when she gave a faint smile, she glowed with maturity. She hoped Taylor wouldn't think she'd spent too much time getting ready. Meg insisted on putting some makeup on her even though Kimmie had never worn anything besides chapstick and blush before. The foundation did wonders at hiding the smudges beneath Kimmie's eyes, but when she met with Taylor she still wanted to look and feel like herself.

Meg had fixed the house phone, and Taylor had called a few minutes earlier to let her know he was running late. Apparently dozens of other hungry Anchorage residents were also in the mood for Chinese, and the wait for takeout would be longer than he'd expected. Kimmie paced the downstairs hallway, trying to calm her nerves, trying to keep from feeling guilty. What kind of daughter goes on a date the week her mother dies?

She hummed one of her mom's Bible tunes. *Surely I am with you always, even to the end of the ages.*

How much longer was Taylor going to take? She'd forgotten to ask Meg how to let him through the iron gate up the driveway. She checked the window every few seconds to see if he was on his way, ready to meet him.

From the living room, Pip let out a squeal. When she got to him, she saw him struggling to separate two cars whose bumpers had gotten stuck together.

"Let me help," she urged, but her brother refused to let either of them go.

"If you give them to me, I can fix it." She felt bad for sounding irritated. It wasn't Pip's fault he got frustrated so easily.

She finally managed to yank the cars out of his hands, ignoring the angry shrieks that died down the moment he realized his toys were free. She wondered what Taylor would think if she tried to wrestle her brother's medicine into him after dinner. It would probably be best to wait until he was gone.

The doorbell rang, and Kimmie sprinted ahead, reaching it in just a few strides. Suddenly feeling foolish, she waited until she caught her breath so Taylor wouldn't think she'd been running, then flung the door open.

The smile froze on her lips.

It wasn't Taylor at the door.

CHAPTER 46

"Hello, Kimmie. You're looking grown-up tonight." Chuck leered at her and shoved his way into the entrance, locking the door behind him.

"What are you doing?" Kimmie could barely stammer the question.

"Just checking up on my favorite stepdaughter." He let out a grating chuckle as he glanced around the foyer. "Too bad you're the ugly one of the sisters. You could never get a rich man to marry you and set you up in a home like this. Not with a face like that."

Kimmie was bombarded with a dozen thoughts at once, which all finally managed to clear their way through the chaos into the single realization: *I have to protect Pip.*

She figured the longer she could keep Chuck here in the foyer with her, the more chance her brother would have of staying safe. Maybe he'd recognize his father's voice and hide. Kimmie wished there was a clock somewhere. If she stalled long enough, Taylor would show up. He'd know what to do.

Deciding that the best way to protect herself and her brother was to keep Chuck as calm as possible, she led him to the kitchen, taking the long route so he wouldn't pass the living room.

"Where's Pip?" Chuck asked, glancing around as if his son might be hiding in one of the kitchen cabinets.

"He's not feeling well. He's got strep throat."

Kimmie eyed the drawer where the meat knife was kept, trying to edge her way closer to it.

"Is that a phone behind you?" he asked with a snarl.

She nodded.

"Unplug it and slide it over to me."

She didn't argue. The movement allowed her to sidle up to the knife drawer, which is where she hoped to stay for the remainder of this conversation.

Chuck slammed the phone against the counter, chuckling as the batteries flew out, then he did the same with the base. "There now." His eyes glinted in the sunlight streaming in from the windows in the vaulted ceiling. "Any other phones I need to know about?"

Kimmie shook her head.

"I suppose you know why I'm here."

Kimmie blinked at him. Why was he here? To kill her? To kidnap Pip? Whatever it was he wanted, he wouldn't succeed. She inched her hand behind her toward the handle of the knife drawer.

"Your sister's got something that belongs to me."

Kimmie didn't know what he was talking about, and she flinched when Chuck snarled, "Where is it?"

"I think it's in her room," she lied, hoping he might turn around, distracted enough to let her get at the knife.

Chuck took a step toward her and grabbed her arm, pinching until she sucked in her breath from the sharp pain. "Take me there."

She took the long way again, praying that God would send his angels to protect Pip. As long as her brother stayed safe, it didn't matter what happened to her.

Halfway up the staircase, she paused and glanced behind.

"Hurry up," Chuck snarled.

She led him into her sister's room.

"Where is it?" he demanded.

"In one of her dressers. She didn't say which."

Chuck started ripping out the drawers of Meg's bureaus, flinging undergarments and shirts and gym clothes across the floor. Kimmie bit her lip. She didn't know what he was looking for, but as long as he stayed busy, nobody would get hurt. She glanced around her sister's room, wondering if there might be another phone in here.

"I don't see it," Chuck growled, flinging the last drawer against the bedpost.

"She said it was in here, I swear it." Kimmie had to keep him distracted. He glowered at her, and she realized the sickening truth. He was sober. This wasn't some kind of drunken rage. This was methodical, premeditated.

Pip, I hope you're hiding somewhere ...

"Stop lying to me and tell me where that brat put it." Chuck stepped toward her, and Kimmie automatically inched her way toward the wall.

"There's another room. Her husband's. I might have made a mistake. It might be in there."

With as many rooms as Meg had in her home, hopefully Chuck's search would keep him busy enough until Taylor arrived or Kimmie found some way to call for help.

She pointed to the door Dwayne had popped out of earlier today, and she marveled that someone like her brother-in-law could have ever frightened her. After what Chuck had already put her through during the past ten years, she should be immune to silly fears.

234

Her legs were steady as he pulled her behind him, striding toward Dwayne's door.

"If you don't find me what I'm looking for, I swear I'll kill you." His voice was low and menacing, and Kimmie had no problem believing every word.

Dwayne's room was different than his wife's. His king-sized bed took up most of the floor space, and the only other furniture was one small end table. Chuck yanked out the drawers, spilling their contents onto the bed. Just a few sports magazines, a bar of deodorant, and a plastic wrapper.

"Where are those blasted letters?" Chuck was bellowing in her face, and Kimmie felt herself shrink as she tried to inch farther and farther away from his fury.

"You think you can get away with hiding them from me like that?" he yelled. "I told you I'd kill you if you didn't hand them over."

He grabbed her hair and yanked down. "You think you're so clever? I'll show you who the smart one is around here."

She shut her eyes as he kneed her in the gut and then the face. Blood spilled from her nose. She tried to swing her arm to push him away, but he grabbed it and kept it pinned behind her back. One small jerk and he could snap her shoulder out of place.

He let his fist fall on her back. She let out a pained gasp as the wind rushed out of her lungs, and Chuck mocked her in his grating falsetto. "Is baby girl hurting? Did precious little princess get a boo-boo?"

Kimmie tried to not to make any noise. Chuck had threatened to kill her in the past, but tonight he clearly possessed the physical stamina and clarity of mind to carry out his plan.

"Tell me where those letters are." His fist found its way to her gut, driving her to her tiptoes with its force.

She collapsed onto the ground, and he straddled her in an instant. *Stupid, stupid, stupid.* What had she been thinking? That she could outwit him? That there was any way to get the upper hand? There was no way to escape this. Chuck wrapped his beefy hands around her throat. He was too strong. She couldn't protect herself. But maybe it was better this way. If Chuck killed her, at least she could join her mom in heaven.

The thought sent a wave of peace spreading through her broken body. As long as she didn't give way again to fear, it was going to be all right.

Warmth flooded her spirit. A peace far more poignant than anything she'd ever known overcame her senses. Her body flailed beneath Chuck's weight, but her physical survival instinct was something separate, something distinct. It wasn't her at all. She watched it as if from above. So this was what it felt like to die. She thought about how many times in the past she had struggled in vain against Chuck and his violent outbursts, striving with a purely animalistic instinct for her own survival. If she'd known death was anything like this, she would have never been so afraid.

I'm going to see my mother again. The realization flooded her with joy, a sense of lasting happiness and contentment unlike anything she'd experienced in the past ten years.

I'm going to be with Jesus soon. No, not even soon. God was here. Right here. Right now. She knew it just as clearly as she knew that once Chuck killed her, she would be in the presence of a Majesty more holy and powerful and personal than any mortal could dare imagine. That glory was hers. It was waiting for her. She could almost hear the sound of her heavenly Father's voice ready to welcome her into paradise.

Somewhere in the distance, Chuck was roaring at her, cursing her as he drained the life out of her with his meaty hands.

Her body seized. Her brain jostled awake. *Wait.* What was she thinking? She couldn't die. She had to help her brother.

She struggled. Strained even though she knew the battle was

already lost.

God, help me. I need to save him.

Chuck's sweat beaded onto his forehead and dripped down on her. She had to get away from him, but it was impossible.

I'm sorry, Pip.

A few more seconds, and it would all be over. Maybe it already was. Through her blurred and blotchy vision, she saw Chuck stand up. He was done?

It was just as well. Just a few more minutes. Then she'd be home.

At the doorway he turned. Something small was in his hands. He aimed it at her.

Kimmie didn't even hear the gun's explosion. Chuck's words and threats meant nothing anymore. She closed her eyes. She was ready to go home.

CHAPTER 47

It was everything her mother told her it would be. The streets were made of glass, the gates of the most exquisite jewels.

He was there. She could sense him even though she didn't see him, the warmth of his fatherly love soothing over any pain, silencing any fears. She wanted to run to him, but something was stopping her.

She didn't understand. She could hear the distant music and wanted to join in the majestic chorus, but she was too far away. She couldn't make out the melody, could only faintly hear it, sense it as a vague echo of what might have been.

It was getting quieter now, fading further off into the distance. Kimmie was frantic to find out what she had to do to get it back.

Is someone there? Is that you, Mom?

The music stopped, and the pain that battered every inch of her body immediately stole away any memory of the joy or peace she had previously felt. It had all been a dream. There was no heavenly bubble of protection, no glorious music, no majestic homecoming.

She was still alive. For all Chuck's threats, he hadn't managed to kill her after all.

Someone was with her, someone watching over her, trying to wake her up.

Mom? Are you here?

As soon as she tried to speak the words, Kimmie remembered her mother was in a different place, the paradise that Kimmie had only managed to glimpse from the other side of an unscalable chasm.

Her mom couldn't help her now. Nobody could.

Kimmie shut her eyes again, wondering just how much longer she'd have to wait before she heard that heavenly music once again.

CHAPTER 48

It was hard to guess how many times Kimmie had drifted in and out consciousness, begging to wake up in the paradise she'd envisioned, only to find herself still lying in a broken heap on a bloodstained carpet. Where was Pip?

That one thought alone gave her reason to try to rouse herself. She had to find out if her brother was okay. Searing pain in her shoulder made crawling impossible, so she used her legs to scoot, inch by inch, collapsing every few feet from the effort. Through the roaring in her ears, she heard the Bible songs her mother used to sing.

I can do all things, I can do all things, I can do all things through him who gives me strength.

She didn't know how far she'd moved. It felt like miles, except she was still in Dwayne's bedroom. She had to make it downstairs. Had to check on Pip.

I can do all things, I can do all things, I can do all things …

Throughout the past ten years, the bulk of Kimmie's prayer

life had been spent asking God to release her and her family from Chuck's tyranny. When the Lord remained silent, she eventually grew tired of asking. But now, the instinct to pray, to plead, to call on the Lord for help, was just as strong as the urge to survive. She had to keep going. Had to make sure her brother was okay. She didn't know the extent of her injuries and wasn't sure if she was putting herself in more danger by trying to move. All she knew was that if Chuck had been angry enough to do this to her, he might have done anything to Pip. She had to find out. And if her brother was still in danger, she would fight her stepfather until her dying breath to keep Pip safe.

Down the hall, a trickle of wet blood following behind her, she pressed on to the staircase.

What now?

She couldn't think about the pain. Couldn't even think about her own survival. All she had to push herself forward was the image of her brother's scared face. She had to get to Pip.

She tried to call out to him, but it hurt too much. She couldn't inhale enough air. She blacked out on the top of the staircase, and when she opened her eyes again, they stung.

Smoke.

She did her best to look behind her but could only turn her head a few degrees before the pain rippled down to her ribs and radiated through her entire body. The smoke was coming from upstairs. She had to go down. She had to get to Pip.

Scooting on her bottom like a tiny toddler pretending the stairs were a giant slide, she grimaced against the pain and worked her way down. She nearly passed out once more on the center step but forced her eyes to stay open even though her mind registered nothing but the pain.

Pip. She had to save Pip.

Whatever Chuck had done, the fire was upstairs. She still had time. She had to save her brother.

At the bottom step, adrenaline soared through her, and she managed a few whole steps before tottering down. Her head was light. The pain in her shoulder made it nearly impossible to focus on anything else.

Help me, God.

She was moving again. It wasn't graceful or efficient, but she struggled forward inch by painstaking inch to the living room, her lungs stinging with every breath she took. Whatever flames upstairs were causing the smoke, she couldn't hear them over the roaring of her pulse in her ears.

Just another ten feet to the living room.

"Pip," she croaked, steeling herself for whatever she might find. Would he be injured too? She had no idea how she'd carry him, but she'd muster the strength to get him out of this house and to safety. That's all that mattered. She might be dead in ten minutes, but as long as she got Pip outside, it would be okay.

She grabbed onto the doorframe and pulled herself forward with a groan.

She was in the living room.

But her brother wasn't there.

CHAPTER 49

Kimmie woke up from another blackout, trying to remember what she was doing on the floor in a room full of smoke.

Someone was calling her name, someone muffled and far away.

Where was Pip?

She tried to push herself up, but there was no connection left between her brain's demands and her body's ability to comply.

"Pip!" She was screaming the word, or at least she thought she was, but she couldn't hear herself.

Smoke stung her lungs. She tried to cough, but the hot pain streaking from her ribs immobilized her completely.

What had Chuck done to Pip?

"Kimmie." She ignored the voice. She had a job to do. She couldn't fail her brother. If only she could remember how to move.

A man's face frowned down at her. Fingers touched her face, but she didn't feel them. He was saying something to her, but she couldn't understand the words. It wasn't until he tried to move her that she fought him off. No, she needed to save Pip. He couldn't take her anywhere.

She thrashed her body, fighting him off, confusion and pain clouding out any higher reasoning. She screamed her brother's name, the first time she'd managed to make her own voice heard.

He whispered something in her ear, but she couldn't hear it over the deafening roar of flames.

CHAPTER 50

Kimmie blinked her eyes open.

"Can you hear me?" A kind face gazed down at her, the relief evident in his eyes.

Her lips were dry and cracking.

"Don't try to talk," he told her. "They're taking you to the hospital. You're going to be all right."

She didn't believe him. He was lying to her. She was dying. There was no way to recover from injuries this severe. And she'd failed to save her brother.

The stretcher she was lying on bounced as it was wheeled down her sister's walkway. Ahead of her she saw the iron gate wide open and wondered how the ambulance had managed to get inside. The stretcher turned as they approached the vehicle, and she saw her sister's home engulfed in flames.

"Pip!" The sound was deafening, a roar of pain and terror and trauma and disbelief. "Pip!" Her soul screamed out the words, but all she could hear were kind assurances from the man beside her.

"Everything's going to be okay." Yet another lie.

The stretcher was hefted into the back of the ambulance. She shut her eyes, but all she could see were the flames that had claimed her brother's life. She hadn't reached him in time. It didn't matter what happened to her now. They might as well let her die as quickly as possible.

She was ready.

There was nothing left for her on earth.

CHAPTER 51

Kimmie woke up to the sound of a muffled conversation.

"… captured right near Northern Lights Boulevard …"

"… arson and attempted murder …"

"… still can't believe how this could have happened."

She opened her eyes. "Hello?"

Her sister was at her bedside in an instant. "You're awake. Hey, over here. She's awake. Someone go get the nurse. Wait, I'll use the call button. Do you need more morphine?"

Kimmie squinted her eyes in the blinding overhead light and wondered if this was how Chuck felt when he woke up with a hangover.

"How are you doing?" Taylor was beside her. There was something familiar about his presence. Memories of smoke and flame flashed in her mind.

"That was you?" Her voice was hoarse and untested, unfamiliar even to herself, but he smiled.

"Yeah. That was me."

"Wasn't he heroic?" Meg crooned.

He reached out and took Kimmie's hand. She squeezed as tightly as she could. She wanted to hear the truth from him. Meg would just ruin it all with her tears and emotionalism. Taylor would tell her the truth. He'd help her accept what happened.

"Was Pip ...?" She couldn't bring herself to finish the question but continued to hang onto him, praying he'd understand.

Taylor glanced at Meg. No, Kimmie wanted to hear it from him. She gave his hand one last, pleading squeeze, and Taylor cleared his throat. "You want to hear everything?"

"I think she should rest," Meg inserted.

Shut up, Kimmie wanted to say but kept her eyes focused on Taylor.

He set his other hand on top of hers. "Pip was in the house when your stepdad started that fire. We think Chuck was looking for letters your mom sent Meg, letters depicting the kind of abuse you and your family suffered, letters indicating she was planning to run away but was afraid if Chuck found out, he'd kill her. He wanted to destroy what evidence he could, and when he didn't find what he was looking for, we can only assume he torched the place in hopes of covering his tracks."

Kimmie didn't care about motive or method. She only wanted to know how much her brother had suffered.

"Pip was a very brave, very smart little boy," Taylor went on. "When I got to your sister's place, I called the fire department and saw you in the living room. I got you out but you were worried about Pip so I went back to look for him. I found him hiding in the bathtub, surrounded by his toy cars."

Kimmie's throat seized in pain when she asked, "Was he hurt?"

Taylor shook his head. "He's doing great. The doctors want to check him out, but from everything we can tell, your stepdad never laid a hand on him. Besides a little smoke inhalation, he's going to be just fine."

CHAPTER 52

Five days later

"Come on, hot stuff. Recovering from shoulder surgery is no excuse to miss your big date." Meg dumped her bag full of cosmetics onto Kimmie's hospital bed. "You know, there's absolutely no way this guy would drive four hours and a half one way on his day off if he wasn't already totally into you. Not to mention the fact that he singlehandedly broke down my door and rushed into a burning building to save your life."

"And Pip's," Kimmie added weakly.

Meg grinned. "Right. And Pip's. Which reminds me, you know that daycare he's been going to? They actually have a worker going on maternity leave in exactly four weeks, which means if you want the job, it's yours."

"Really?"

"Yeah, but you can thank me later. Right now, I just need you to shut your eyes so I don't poke you with my liner. No, don't scrunch them up like that. Just look down. Like this."

252

"Did anyone ever tell you that you're bossy?"

"Thank you. Oh, speaking of bossy, you're not going to forget to ask him about that prescription, are you? You can learn a lot about a man by what drugs he takes."

"No, I'm not going to ask about his prescription. That's his business."

Meg shrugged. "Well, then, don't come whining to me when you find out he's got some fatal illness right when things are starting to get serious. Or have you ever considered that he could have an STD?"

"Will you cut it out?" Kimmie snapped.

"Fine. Fine. Now are you going to let me do your makeup or what? This man risked his life to save you. The least you could do in return is let me make you presentable."

Four days later

"So you ready to be back home? Or at least back at your sister's?" Taylor asked.

Kimmie held the hospital phone close to her ear in order to hear better over the sound of Pixar's *Cars* playing loudly on the TV. "Yeah. It'll be good to spend more time with Pip."

"Is he enjoying that daycare?"

"Yeah. It's a really nice place. I've talked to the director there a few times. She said her daughter was a lot like Pip, didn't talk for the first few years, things like that, and now she's a senior at Dimond High and planning to become a speech pathologist."

"That's awesome. Hey, is Pip there with you now?"

"Yeah."

"Let me talk to the little Buster."

Kimmie called Pip over, wincing when he jostled her injured shoulder as he made his way to his perch on her pillow, his favorite seat in her hospital room. "Trooper Taylor wants to say hi."

She handed him the phone and could hear Taylor's voice on the other end. "Hi, buddy. Are you having a good day?"

Pip stared at the receiver then ran his favorite car up and down it.

"What's that noise?" Taylor asked. "What's he doing?"

"He's driving his car on the mouthpiece," Kimmie explained. Giving her brother a kiss, she brought the phone back to her ear.

"That was one of our best conversations yet," Taylor joked.

"I think he likes you."

"Yeah?" Even across the miles, she could hear the grin in Taylor's voice. "What makes you think that?"

"That was his favorite car. If he didn't like you he would have used the dump truck."

Twelve days later

Meg stood at the top of the staircase, shaking her head. "No. Absolutely not."

Kimmie looked down at herself. "What's wrong?"

"Nobody goes to La Mesa's in flats and a plain brown sweater."

"You're the one who gave me this plain brown sweater."

"And it'd be fine if he were taking you out for McDonalds. This is La Mesa. Sheesh. Super high-end."

"I didn't know."

Meg rolled her eyes. "You've got to keep up with the times. Now go change"

Kimmie glanced at her clothes. "But I like this sweater."

Meg rolled her eyes. "Sometimes I think you're totally hopeless. You have no idea how into you this guy is. First he saves your life, then he spends every single day off driving all the way out here to take you to the fanciest restaurants in Anchorage. How clueless do you have to be?"

"About as clueless as the woman who didn't know her husband was having an affair with the office assistant?"

Meg waved her hand in the air dismissively as she hurried down the stairs. "Touché. But I did know about it, for the record. I just didn't want to say anything until we'd been married five years. And the timing couldn't have been better. I'm getting my share of the insurance money from the fire, and he can have the rest. Including Miss Secretary. And hey, if Taylor wants you to sign any prenups before you guys tie the knot, tell me and I'll have my lawyer look it over for you. That guy literally saved my life."

Kimmie rolled her eyes. "It's our second date. The only knots I'm working on right now are the ones in the back of my head. Even with the physical therapy, I can't manage to reach back there to get it brushed out."

"That's what you have me for. That and making sure you don't walk into La Mesa's looking like a thrift-store special. Come on. Let's get you back to your room. I hate to say it, but we have a lot more work to do. By the way, did Officer Hard Abs ever respond to your text? What did he say?"

"It wasn't *my* text, and I'm still mad at you for stealing my phone like that. You had no right, you know."

Meg pulled Kimmie into her bathroom and started attacking her hair with a brush. "Ok. Sorry, not sorry. Now what did he say? Did he tell you what meds he's on?"

"Actually, he told me he takes nothing but a multivitamin."

"What about his prescription he picked up from the pharmacy?" Meg was yanking her hair mercilessly, but Kimmie still wanted to stretch the story out a little longer. Her sister deserved it.

"The day we ran into him in the clinic, he was picking up flu medicine for a little old lady who was too sick to leave her home."

Meg stopped assaulting her with the brush and stared into the mirror. "Seriously? You're not pulling my leg?"

Kimmie grinned. "I might be. Guess you'll never know, will you?"

Meg reached into Kimmie's pocket. "But I can look at your phone, can't I?"

Kimmie giggled as she tried to push her sister away. "You can try, but I already deleted the text."

"I should have never taught you how to use a cell."

"You should have never texted my boyfriend and asked about his personal business."

"Wait, he's visited you at the hospital and he's taking you out to dinner at La Mesa's, and he's your boyfriend all of a sudden?"

Kimmie smiled and shrugged. "Yeah. A lot can change in

two weeks. You've got to keep up with the times."

Three hours later

"You're looking lovely." Taylor raised his water goblet and smiled at her warmly.

"Thanks."

"How's Pip?"

"He's great. He had his first meeting with the new speech therapist yesterday. She's been working with kids like him for almost twenty years, and she specializes in the four and under age range, so I think it's going to be a perfect match."

"Speaking of perfect matches," he said, reaching for her hand, "I'm really glad we've been able to spend this time together."

She smiled back at him. "Me, too." Kimmie still didn't understand what Taylor saw in her, but it must be something since he was calling her every day on her new cell phone and making plans to drive to Anchorage to see her on almost all of his upcoming weekends.

"I know we weren't going to discuss the trial at dinner, but I did want to tell you they set the date."

"What's that mean?"

"For right now, nothing. Even without your testimony,

they're already building up a solid case. Everyone's sounding pretty confident he'll be tried not only for the house fire and your assault but for your mom's murder as well."

Kimmie wondered if she'd ever get used to hearing the words *mom* and *murder* together. With everything that had happened — her injuries coupled with her long physical recovery plus the relief at having Pip safe — she was still processing her mom's death in choppy spurts and pieces. She was grateful that Taylor felt comfortable with her sudden bursts of emotion, grateful to finally have someone to talk to, someone who allowed her to feel secure enough to be her true self. Until she met Taylor, she wasn't even sure she knew who that was.

The waiter in his flawless tuxedo served their appetizer dish, and Taylor took both her hands in his. "Shall we pray?"

She nodded. In spite of all she and her family had gone through, there were still hundreds of reasons to give thanks.

CHAPTER 53

Spring

The Copper River Basin had broken out into spring, the season where the roads turned to slush as the snow melted, leaving acres of puddles and perfect breeding conditions for raising next summer's batch of mosquitoes.

Kimmie was nervous. It wasn't her first trip back to Glennallen. She'd already returned to speak several times with the prosecuting attorney assigned to her stepfather's murder and arson trial. She was also here last Christmas, when Taylor drove her out so she could attend his work Christmas party and meet all the colleagues he'd talked so much about. But this was the first time she'd step foot in Chuck's old trailer since the night she and Pip fled through the woods.

"You sure you want to do this?" Taylor asked, holding his arm protectively around her waist.

She nodded. After Kimmie healed from her physical wounds, her sister talked her into trying out the same counselor

Meg had seen after slitting her wrists. Kimmie had balked at the idea, but Meg had so many nice things to say about the woman and wouldn't stop nagging, so Kimmie finally agreed.

Half a year later, she was still seeing the same therapist, who agreed that this one last pilgrimage home could play a large role in Kimmie's healing process.

She was glad to have Taylor with her and glad that Meg had taken time off her new job as a fitness director to watch Pip. After spending the day with Taylor, Kimmie would head over to Jade's and crash on her friend's couch before Taylor drove her back to Anchorage tomorrow. With as close as they'd become over the months, it was surprising to think that this was the longest stretch of time she'd spent with him without either her sister or Pip around.

He gave her a reassuring squeeze. "Want me to wait out here?"

She shook her head, certain that there would be no way she could confront these memories of her past if Taylor weren't here with her.

"Got your letter?" he asked.

She took the single sheet of paper out of her pocket and unfolded it. When she and her therapist had come up with this idea, Kimmie thought she'd be too embarrassed to read something out loud, but now with Taylor here by her side, she felt safe.

She could do this.

The trailer was almost exactly like she'd left it. Nobody had come to clean it out. There was Chuck's recliner, with the trash and litter he'd left there before he went after Kimmie and her brother in Anchorage.

There were the used napkins on the floor. If she walked into the kitchen, she was certain she'd find the same pile of dirty dishes in the sink that she'd left there the night she ran away.

But she didn't need to go that far. Everything she wanted to do could take place right here in the living room.

She spread out her letter and with trembling hands began to read.

Dear Chuck, to say you ruined my teen years and early adult life would be a gross understatement. Because of you, I lived in constant fear, hunger, and emotional turmoil. I wasn't able to form any meaningful friendships with others my age because I was too afraid to let anyone get close, embarrassed to think that someone might discover the squalor and terror in which we lived.

Your abuse touched every aspect of my life, and as a result I lacked confidence and never felt like I had any sense of control over my future, my will, or my body. The fact that you killed my mother and then blamed her death on suicide has haunted me for months. I've lost untold hours of sleep and am afraid of the dark now because of you. Even worse is the way you treated my brother. No child should have to grow up knowing his own father is a heartless murderer.

But in spite of all the ways you deprived Pip of the things a healthy child needs to mature, he is thriving without you. With his speech therapist's help, he's stringing words together now and knows over three dozen signs. If your goal was to make your son as miserable as you made me, you have already failed. He is happier, healthier, and better off without you.

I wasn't exaggerating when I said you ruined my life, but just like I refuse to watch you hurt your son anymore, I also refuse to let you ruin or dictate my future. The coping mechanisms I learned while I was under your roof were survival instincts that helped me endure life in your home, but I don't need to rely on those bad habits anymore. I am surrounded by a vivacious and fun-loving sister, an adorable little brother, and a boyfriend who has supported me through each and every step of my healing journey.

I suppose if I had the time and the energy, I could sit and ask you why you did the things you did. If you despised the person you were just as much as you made us despise you, if there was a deep sadness or trauma in your past that made you turn into the monster you became. But I don't want to know those answers. And I don't want to ask you those questions.

I forgive you for what you've done to me and my family. I forgive you, but that doesn't mean I'm free from anger. It's something I know I need to pray about more, and it might be something that takes a lifetime to heal from. This is my journey. I'm far from whole, but I'm thankful that my family and I can finally live in peace.

And maybe the more I heal, the more forgiveness I can find in my heart toward you for all you did.

Kimmie glanced up at Taylor when she finished reading. What was supposed to happen now? What should they say?

He leaned down and kissed her on the forehead. "That was perfect. I'm so proud of you."

He took her hand in his and squeezed. "Before we go, I have a letter of my own."

CHAPTER 54

Kimmie was surprised when Taylor took a folded piece of paper out of his own pocket.

"What are you doing?" she asked.

"You'll see." His voice was loud, stronger than hers, when he started to read.

"*Dear Mrs. Jenkins, I'm Taylor, and I'm so sorry that we never had the privilege of meeting in this life. I have, however, had the privilege of dating your daughter now for almost nine months, and I'm sure you already know this, but she is a true delight. She's made my life so full, and I'm a better man for the time we've spent together. She's also told me what a great mother you were, and in a way, I feel like I already know you.*

"*That's why I hope that if you really were alive you'd give your blessing to what I'm about to ask. See, I want to make Kimmie my wife, but my mama raised me old-fashioned and told me I had to get the parents' permission before asking a girl to marry me. Since we all know that a solid marriage isn't based just on how poetically you can claim your love for someone, I'd like to tell you what my prospects are.*

"I'm a trooper living in Glennallen, but that's caused a few problems for Kimmie and me. See, she's in Anchorage, where she's got a great job and where Pip is getting all these fabulous services, so I really can't find it in me to ask her to uproot herself from all that and come back here where she'll be met by so many painful memories. And I doubt your daughters would admit it, but I think Kimmie and Meg would miss each other if I tried to tear them apart.

"Which is why I ended up getting a new position lined up, and I'll be starting at the Anchorage police academy in six weeks. Assuming your daughter says yes, I'd like to make her my wife sometime this summer. I might not be able to afford a mansion on the hillside, but I'd like to see her settled into a nice house, her and Pip both, and I'd just like to mention that if the opportunity comes and it feels like the timing's right, I would consider it a blessing and an honor to officially adopt your son because I love that little boy, and I'm already so proud of the developments he's made.

"To be quite honest, Mrs. Jenkins, I've been meaning to find a way to ask your daughter to marry me for quite some time now, and being the big chicken I am, this is the best idea I could

come up with. I promise that if she agrees to my proposal, I'll spend every day providing for her, protecting her, and giving Pip the happy childhood a boy like him deserves."

Kimmie stared up when Taylor finished reading. Was he actually shaking?

He folded the paper up and tucked it back into his pocket. "Well?" he asked.

She stood up on her tiptoes and wrapped her arms around his neck. "Of course," she whispered and melted into his kiss.

A NOTE FROM THE AUTHOR

Termination Dust could have never been written if I hadn't spent years living in rural (and I do mean rural!) Alaska.

One of the scariest parts of life out here for me as a mom was how far we were from medical care. At one point my son had a hard time catching his breath (and even stopped breathing entirely). It took almost an hour on the road to get him to the clinic, then another couple hours to fly him on a med-evac flight to Anchorage.

Thankfully, he was fine, and the adventure turned into something I could write about later.

Because lots of suspenseful things can happen when you live in a region with more bears and moose than humans!

Speaking of Alaska-based suspense, if you're ready for another adrenaline rush, you can dive right into *Frost Heaves*, another Alaskan Refuge Christian suspense novel.

After escaping a dangerous cult when she was a teen, Jade has learned to turn her life around. No, with the temperatures dropping and the clock ticking, Jade will do anything to find her missing daughter. She'll risk her own life ... or even someone else's to be reunited with her little girl.

If you liked the intensity and excitement about Kimmie's struggle to keep her brother safe, you'll love everything about Jade's quest to rescue her kidnapped daughter ... and ensure that justice gets served.

For a suspense novel that readers are calling intense, heart-pounding, and impossible to put down, read *Frost Heaves* today.